Letters From

Al

To Jean,

Happy Reading

hope you enjoy a

Nebraska mystery!

Kathy Peeper

WhoooDoo Mysteries
A division of
Treble Heart Book

WhoooDoo Mysteries
a division of
Treble Heart Books
1284 Overlook Dr.
Sierra Vista, AZ 85635-5512
http://www.trebleheartbooks.com

Published and Printed in the U.S.A.

ISBN: 978-1-936127-47-4
1-936127-47-4
LCCN: 2011926663

Thank you for choosing another WhoooDoo Mysteries Selection

Dedication

To my husband and computer technician, David, and to Heide Aken, my web mistress, and, of course, to Great Aunt Sophia 1902 - 2004.

Letters From Al

by

Kathleen Pieper

WhoooDoo Mysteries

A division of

Treble Heart Books

Prologue

Chicago, 1925

The damp pavement reflected the slight figure of a lone young woman walking down Carroll Street. She hurried, glancing over her shoulder fearfully at the fast darkening sky.

"Late again, Edna's going to fire me for sure." She said to herself, looking for courage in the shadows that moved around her.

She passed darkened buildings on deserted streets, wishing she could see in as an occasional door would quickly open and close. The sound of clinking glasses and laughter accompanied by music slipping out from the illegal Chicago clubs known as Speakeasies always secretly fascinated the young woman.

She tried to get a glimpse in, only to be met with furtive glares from sinister eyes. The exciting stories she read in the newspapers of Chicago's reputation for murder and mayhem made for big headlines and dubious fame. It also made her heart beat faster at the hint of mystery and excitement going on.

For over a year she had hidden, living on her own. Her money soon ran out and she got a job as a waitress by day while she dreamed of studying art in Paris by night. It was a scandalous plan for the times, one her relatives did not approve of. It had been the turning point of her decision, to run away.

Madeline took a deep breath. The night air was crisp and cool. An excitement and eagerness filled her with anticipation at the thrill of being young and on her own. Finally free of that stuffy mansion on the hill, full to the brim of bossy, snobbish relatives always telling her what to do.

That was then. Madeline gave a little skip and continued down the street becoming aware of shadows darting in and out from the alley across the street from the diner. Quickly she shrank against the damp brick building. Ducking behind the trash bins with her heart pounding, she heard static whispers.

"He's in there, I tell you. Let's just get it done." The voice whined.

"No. I told you we got to do it right. We don't want no witnesses and we don't want no *coppers*. We can't be sure about some of them in this part of town." The second man was cool and collected. The first man cursed under his breath and looked around nervously.

"Damn. We're going to a lot of trouble to get rid of

Capone. With that scar on his face, anyone could pick him out of a crowd and ice him."

"Quiet. There. There, that's him all right, at the back of the diner. We'll get him when he comes out. Let him eat his meal, his last meal. Now shut up and get across the street, we'll get him in a crossfire. Mr. Moran will like that." The laughter was pure evil. When they moved, Madeline realized they would see her.

There was no time to think. With dry lips, she managed to blow what she hoped sounded like a casual whistle and started walking down the street. There was more movement in the alley but she pretended not to notice. Passing near a large trash can, she kicked it over and knocked the lid to the ground where it rattled noisily.

"Ouch." She feigned a soft cry and bent over. The two men stepped out of the shadows but their menacing scowls turned into lusty grins when they saw a young pretty woman, her skirt high showing off a pair of shapely legs. A red mark she made with her fingernail only seconds before came across nicely as a scratch from the lid.

"Darn it, all. I'm just so clumsy, but you startled me." Giving a wide-eyed, slightly scared look, she smiled a pouty smile she learned from the cinema. Licking her lips reddened with lip rouge, she batted her eyelashes innocently at the two thugs, hoping it worked as well for her as it had for the heroine. They looked surprised but smiled back.

"I'm just on my way to work and I think I'm late." She lied and smiled sweetly at them although shaking like a leaf on the inside.

"Well, you shouldn't be out here all alone, pretty thing like you. Never know what's waiting for you in the dark. Best you get going."

"Thanks, mister." She let her skirt drop and looked coyly over her shoulder, giving a flirty wave.

They watched her cross the street and gave each other an uneasy glance, melting back into the shadows.

A scar. The man said he, Capone, had a scar on his face. Madeline reached the diner feeling as if she had a bulls-eye painted on her back. But no bullets whizzed by her. *Now what?* Taking her coat off and glancing out the large plate glass window, she debated on what to do next. Should she tell Edna or approach Capone?

The infamous gangster, Al Capone sat reading a menu with another man in the last booth in the narrow diner. Frowning at her being late again, the cook nodded for her to take their order. Taking a deep breath Madeline looked around at the innocent people in the diner and knew what she had to do. Deliberately dropping her pencil, she bent down beside the gangsters. The words came spilling out.

"There are two men with guns across the street waiting for you, if you're Al Capone." A strange expression crossed the man's face and he straightened up. The round-faced man indeed had a distinctive scar on his face. Eyes wide, his companion flinched, glaring at her.

"She could be lying, Al." The other man kept his hand in his pocket, a menacing look on his face. Al Capone lit his cigar and looked over at her again.

"Are you lying to me, girly?"

Madeline shook her head emphatically. "I do not lie. I just don't want to see anyone get hurt."

"Well, you got an honest face. Okay, girly, just keep smiling. Is that the back door?"

Madeline nodded, her knees quaking.

"What's your name?" Capone paused while his companion looked around nervously.

"Madeline, I mean, Mary. Mary Morris." She suddenly realized she didn't want a well-known gangster knowing her real name.

"Mary or Madeline, then, thanks. I'll remember your good deed." He tipped his hat to her.

"There's no need in that, Sir." She answered stiffly, frightened by even being this close to a gangster. How silly she had ever been to think this life exciting.

"Oh, but there is," he said and winked before disappearing out the back door.

The feeling of dread never left her after that. It even overshadowed the fear of discovery by her family. The next day she was walking home when the man who had been with Al Capone was waiting in front of her building.

"I've got something for you, Miss Morris." He was acting nice but his eyes were cold and suspicious. He put a manila envelope in her hands.

"What's this?" She said primly.

"This is just a 'thank you' for your help the other night. Mr. Capone always pays his debts in full." He turned to go.

With shaking hands Madeline opened the envelope and found money, lots of money. "Wait." She called out, "I can't take this. Here," she thrust it back at him.

Chapter 1
Present Day

"Well? Shall we set the date?" A peck on the cheek and it was business as usual. "After we're married maybe we can take a little trip to see the place."

"Larry, you just can't just dismiss me like this. You think what I want is ridiculous. That means you think I'm ridiculous. How can you say that?" Maddy Morris felt her cheeks grow hot and stubbornly refused to be pushed this time. "I want to go back to Nebraska. When I got the letter about Aunt Madeline, it made me think back about things. Family things I hadn't thought of for a long time."

"What do you mean? You have your Uncles, they tell me they're very fond of you."

"What do my uncles have to do with this conversation? When have you talked to my uncles about me?" Maddy flared back, warning lights going off in her head. She did not want her uncles knowing her business. The resistance grew, trust of Larry didn't.

"Well, they're sort of my bosses' now, I told you I've moved up in accounting and they, well, they came to me to help you with the shares your parents had and things. The annual stockholders meeting is coming up and they thought you might be confused about how to handle your shares."

"What business is it to them? They never came around before my father died unless it was to get his proxies. They think I'm so dumb I can't vote properly? What is going on, Larry?"

"Maddy, they never said you were dumb. I just think you need some help managing your money. My goodness, what are we arguing about anyway, they only want to help and so do I."

"Look, Larry, I don't like the things I'm hearing about you and my uncles. I can't marry someone I can't trust, the engagement is off. I'm going to Nebraska and that's all there is to it. I think you should leave."

She needed space. The Nebraska letter was perfectly timed, and she needed to go. A neat, curt note again declining his cavalier offer of marriage lay on the hall table the next morning with the ring. Her roommate, Marie would be sure to give it to him. Larry wouldn't be able to change her mind this time. Allowing she didn't have much money, she felt good about her decision as she drove out of town.

The proposal had been a classic chess move, a last resort to keep her under control. Everything was starting to make sense now. Larry was more interested in his job and money than how she felt. She didn't mind that the ring was small, but it felt more like a prop in a grand production with her as the court jester. What a joke, a sad joke. She had almost fallen for it, but not any more. Apparently Larry thought she was so crazy over him that handling her was a done deal. She had seen the family ruin her parents life, they weren't going to ruin hers.

"I can do this. I can read a map for crying out loud," she muttered under her breath as she drove. But she seriously doubted anything she did since last week. Talking to herself had become a habit for her, a way of rationalizing things she would have discussed with her parents or family if she had any she could trust. It was when she missed her parents the most. She could always talk to them.

Even her co-workers encouraged her to get out from behind the stack of books and start living again. But her lack of self-confidence with the opposite sex gravitated from non-existent to awful, especially as of late. It was as if a piece of her heart was missing. Something in her was incomplete.

Maddy thought back to her latest boyfriend, Larry Preston, actually her ex-fiancée. A manipulative but very good-looking guy, who didn't realize being engaged meant you didn't date other girls. He was only the latest jerk in a string of bad choices. It was one of the reasons she had taken off on this pie-in-the-sky road trip, to put a little space between them and do some serious thinking.

The envelope from Jack Drake and Associates from Omaha, Nebraska, had arrived with the news that she was the beneficiary of an inheritance from a long-lost relative. Her father's favorite, eccentric, aunt from the past that she'd completely forgotten about.

After a few calls she found the will had been probated

and she was indeed the heir to her great aunt's estate in Nielsen, Nebraska. If she was the great-niece of Mrs. Madeline O'Keefe, she needed to show proof of birth and claim her inheritance. With her friends clucking at her in the background, she called, claimed, and climbed into the rent-a-Honda, since her little Buick was in hock at the repair shop.

This was when Larry Preston showed his true colors.

To her astonishment, it seemed Larry had been advised by her uncles to find out about this situation and report back to them. They were actually his bosses. Her anger only was greater than the shock of realizing the man you were supposed to have no secrets from, one who could be trusted and share a life with, was dishonest and greedy.

By accident they had switched cell phones one night and that was how Maddy then found out Larry was not only dishonest but unfaithful. His secretary called and left a not-so-discreet message on the phone. Thinking it was her phone, Maddy answered and found out Larry was also a cheater.

He even had the gall to act like it was no big deal. That was the last straw. Maddy had decided it was the perfect time to break it off with him. Investigating this windfall herself would be the perfect way to get her life in order. With the money from her parents estate tied up in the family business, she could use a little extra cash. So far, she hadn't done so well with men.

From what she remembered, Great Aunt Madeline had been kind, but cool and classy even if she was a bit old-fashioned. Maddy recalled her Chicago relatives more. Most of them had never met Aunt Madeline. As she grew up and the years passed, the closeness dwindled, especially after Great Grandmother Morris died and the family business became a corporation. The old ways died along with her, except for the greed.

If things worked out perhaps she'd have enough to start over again. Maybe she'd buy a bookstore or something else exciting and interesting. Larry had been against her even contacting anyone or coming here, preferring she let the local attorney get what money was there and send it on to him/them. He'd invest it for her, he informed her. For the first time she had resisted his advice and now, here she was, alone on the Interstate.

"Where'd you get your license, at a discount store?" She yelled fruitlessly after a big rig swept by her, shaking her hand in frustration. A rest stop appeared out of nowhere and darting in, she breathlessly landed in the last parking spot.

Sweat trickled down making her shirt stick uncomfortably to her back. The air-conditioner was on full blast but only now did she notice it was blowing warm air, not cool.

"Great. That's all I need in the middle of the Nebraska summer, no air." She twisted knobs and pushed levers but to no avail. Resting her head on the steering wheel in defeat she noticed the envelope had blown onto the floor.

"This is all thanks to you and my own greed, thank you very much. I should have known better when I saw it was from an attorney. What am I doing out here in the middle of nowhere?" She stuffed the letter in her pocket and got out of the rented economy car, kicking the front tire with the remaining energy she had left.

"That definitely wasn't worth it," Madeline said through gritted teeth, holding her throbbing toe. Her impatience often got her in trouble. Her Dad used to tease her it was all that red hair. Thinking of him made her smile, feel sad, but still smile. If he and her mom were still alive she wouldn't have to deal with this.

She hopped on one foot for a moment until she realized she was the main attraction for the rest stop crowd and limped into the women's restroom. After splashing cold water on her face, she felt a little better and went out to look around at the tourist information.

She bought a coke from the pop machine and was immediately accosted by a pretty Blonde with a big, too-cheerful smile.

"Where you from?"

"Chicago." Madeline replied tonelessly without looking up from the giant map. She had just found a yellow arrow that said, "You, are here," when the Blonde told her the same thing.

"Okay, I'm here, but where is Nielsen, Nebraska?" Maddy had directed the question to the guide but got no reply. Blonde guide was now immersed in a lecture of the Oregon Trail with a hunky-looking guy from Detroit.

"Abandoned again," Maddy said and sighed, thinking of her ex-boyfriend and her life in general.

Using her finger and following the yellow sticker detour sign, there was Nielsen, Nebraska, fifty miles to go. Relief flooded her and even her toe stopped throbbing. She might make it yet.

All the thoughts and fears she had as she started out on this ill-conceived trip were coming to pass. The fight with her boyfriend, Larry, had started it. People telling her what to do, her friends and her fiancée, it was all terribly frustrating.

"Thanks for stopping by. I think you'll have a wonderful

time in Nebraska." The Blonde guide gushed and batted her eyelashes furiously at Mr. Detroit and Maddy walked out of the building.

"I sure hope you're right." Maddy said under her breath, and smiled back. She threw the brochure in the backseat with all her other stuff. The letter she just stared at. Hefting it in her hand she stared at the formal raised print from a law office. Her name and address looked official in bold black letters. Was she crazy for going off on what could be a wild goose chase?

"Well, my life can't get any more screwed up than it is already, so what have I got to lose?" She shoved the letter back in her pocket and started the car. Turning off the hot, air conditioning, she opened all the windows. Carefully backing out of the busy rest stop she pulled back on the Interstate with renewed hope. Here I come, Nielsen, Nebraska.

Nebraska was really flat, and so hot and dry. She tried to remember how long it had been since she'd been here. She shook her head feeling bad she couldn't. She was a city girl now, skyscrapers and wall-to-wall people. She lived right in the middle of the city, close to the public library where she worked. Yes, this was really different than the Chicago scene.

This was practically desolate, although the little valleys that appeared every so often were pretty, with green pastures, cattle and horses grazing and the little towns visible from the off-ramps.

"I wonder if anyone that I know is still living here. And my first boyfriend, what was his name, Alec? No, he's probably moved away by now if he was smart. Nothing was there then, and I doubt much has changed. Well, except that first kiss. That I remember."

It was easy to daydream about her brief stop in Nebraska years before with the radio not working any better than the air conditioner. She realized she was talking to herself again.

"Get a grip, Girl," she chided herself. Seeing a sign that said "Nielsen 12 miles", she could have wept with relief. "Thank you, thank you." Eagerly she headed down a two-lane highway to a trip back to her childhood, the thing that had made her decide to come to Nielsen personally. There had to be more to her life.

Daydreaming about the time she and her folks came through Nebraska and stayed with her elderly great-aunt, made the miles go faster. Only a few vehicles passed her on the two-lane blacktop, a school bus, a tractor pulling a huge wagon of hay bales, and some pick-ups.

Had it only been a few days since she left Chicago? Had she ever really lived here? Was Nielsen High School still around the corner from the post office? And the all important one, where was her first crush, Alec McKay? Answers to questions she'd never expected to ask herself, now were important.

The unexpected letter that arrived had started it. Somewhere inside her she hoped this letter might change things. Maddy tried to press it flat on the seat beside her, smoothing out the crinkles from being smashed in her pocket. It was twelve years ago, and she was enrolled in her first year of High School. One semester amidst a number of unsettled times for her parents before they gave up trying to make it on their own, and went back to a meaningless job in the lucrative family-owned publishing business in Chicago.

But giving up meant they had to rely on family, family that liked to keep everyone in their place and under the thumb of Grandmother Morris. But she never controlled Aunt Madeline. Stories about her were only whispered in the family because she had defied her grandmother.

She barely recalled her father's favorite aunt, actually her great-aunt, who had settled in the little town of Nielsen, Nebraska, and convinced her parents into moving there, too. Aunt Madeline begged Maddy's father to stick it out, not let the other family members tell them what to do. But, her mother had been sickly and with the cost of medical care, it hadn't been enough.

Her father loved his aunt and he often talked fondly about her in later years. But he also needed the security of a job and he had that back in Chicago. He understood Grandmother Morris was protecting her way of life and the family business in the stern way she had been brought up. He also could empathize with Aunt Madeline's views of independence and being an individual. When Maddy's parents moved back home, they were relegated to acceptable status within the family, but not favored.

Madeline was in her 60s then, with rich red hair in a funny hairdo. Everyone in town called her 'Aunt Madeline'. Stubborn but fair, with a kind and friendly personality, she especially doted on Maddy. With a trace of guilt Maddy remembered thinking how old-fashioned her father's dear aunt was, but in all fairness, it seemed so long ago. The thing Maddy did remember was her first boyfriend, and she'd had to leave him behind along with a good portion of her heart.

Today Alec would probably be considered a hunk. Even then he was sweet natured, handsome, golden haired, captain of the football team. All the girls liked Alec, but he had asked her to her first big dance. She hadn't wanted to leave, and they had promised to write faithfully. She wrote every day for months. He called at first and then, after one letter, he disappeared like a mist, leaving what was left of her young heart broken.

"So much for true love, huh?" She said sarcastically to herself, dodging a farm dog that chased her little blue Honda.

Recalling the pang of first love was still sharp even though it had been a long time ago. It actually made her mad all over again. Brushing damp bangs from her forehead she checked the rearview mirror and watched as the dog gave up in a cloud of dust behind her.

"I wonder if he's married. He'd have a beautiful wife and kids by now. I bet he has a house in the country and two cars. Maybe he's a doctor or lawyer-type. That would be just my luck."

Another water tower loomed up ahead with the name *Nielsen* printed on it. The street names were commonplace, Maple, Elm, Main.

"Okay, now I just need to find one eleven Main Street, Nielsen, Nebraska."

Seeing a tall church steeple ahead, she felt the excitement grow. Just like her great-aunt's house, the town had remained homey and quaint. A statue of a Civil War soldier stood on a pedestal in the town square surveying the area. It stood proudly surrounded by flowers, shrubs and sidewalks, other streets ultimately scattering off into the half dozen side streets filled with other well-kept homes. Surprisingly the town had grown and as she drove in, she'd noticed a large subdivision of neat, modern homes being built. Her aunt's house sat in an older section of town, further back than the others on the lot with a large yard and old-fashioned wrought-iron fence surrounding it.

The old house loomed large and silent in the afternoon light as she drove by slowly to get a look. Maddy stared thoughtfully, trying to remember it. Somehow she thought it would be different, even bigger. As a child it seemed huge, but now, it was roomy, just the right size. Of course any house was larger and more impressive than her apartment.

"You know, I think I could get used to this. Imagine, having a home of my own and not a cramped apartment with a part-time roommate."

As she looked at her aunt's home she got an odd, familiar feeling gazing at the old, two-story, white frame Victorian. With black gingerbread trim and shutters and a porch running the length of the front, it looked cared for even though one shutter hung by a hinge. The lawn furniture lay stored haphazardly against the porch wall. The lawn was a bit scraggly, but cut, and for the most part, well maintained. It looked comfortable and homey.

The funny feeling came over her again. Warmth that she wasn't used to enveloped her. Was it a welcome home? Hardly, she'd lived here such a short time. She brushed it off and parked in front.

"Oh, brother, what am I trying to do? I need to keep a clear head and not read something into all these feelings." Her imagination was leading her into a romanticized version of her childhood. Her parents loved her, which had been enough. Why was she so afraid of being disappointed? She got out and stretched. The drive from Omaha seemed endless and she was bursting with questions and feelings about what to do next. Hands on her hips, she gave the place a good once over.

"Ready or not, here I come. Not to sound greedy, but I wonder just how much you're worth today. Before I start counting my chickens, I better find where the realty office is. The letter said down the street and near the town square. I should be able to find that."

Maddy turned around casting an interested eye at her new surroundings, vague memories surfaced. She finally recalled her directions to the center of town and frowned, wondering if she should walk or drive. Slinging her purse over one shoulder she started out walking, she'd had enough driving for today.

An older woman sat rocking and staring from the porch of the home next door. A cheerful flower garden and vine-covered archway connected the two properties, and was well-used according to the worn path.

The thought made her chuckle. "If you think this outfit is bad, you ought to see my roommate's wardrobe," she said under her breath, thinking of Marie's flamboyant outfits. She was surprised that she didn't miss her roommate that much. Marie could be very bossy at times and with her mild nature, Maddy would always let her have her way. Had she finally had her fill?

Maddy couldn't explain how free and unencumbered she felt now that she was actually here. Nielsen, Nebraska, population 4,500 was a small town in Nebraska, her great aunt's home. Could it be a home for her? She didn't even know if she owned anything yet, and she didn't care. She was here, making her own decisions. Free to go, free to stay if she wanted. The giddiness of choice was invigorating. She might just hang around a little while, the place looked really interesting and the feelings, the memories were starting to return as well.

"I better find out what is involved and not linger over memories too much. That won't pay the bills." She stepped up her pace.

"Well, Aunt Madeline, here I am the unknown niece who carries on the family's black sheep bloodline as well as your name. I wonder if I am as brave as you." She looked down the road at the small town's main street. Festive flags on the streetlights waved in the breeze.

She wondered aloud, with a sigh, "I must be. I'm here."

Chapter 2

Maddy gave one last look over her shoulder at the house on Main Street and picked up her pace. She needed to find the realtor next. Dozens of questions were forming in her mind, mostly about owning a home. She knew it was a big responsibility and wondered how expensive it would be to heat and cool. How much the taxes were, practical things.

Her friends kept saying things would work out but Maddy was never sure. Right now her car was in the shop and her dentist had sent a letter threatening to repossess the last crown in her mouth. Yes, the money was part of it. She was tired of being broke. So, it hadn't taken her long to realize this might be her way out.

"People from Illinois always talk to themselves?" An amused voice broke her train of thought.

Startled, she jumped at the deep voice coming from

behind her. A handsome, suntanned face peered at her, and a wide grin greeted her through an open car window. The face was vaguely familiar. There was a flashing red light on top of the car, and a big silver badge painted on the side. The officer wore a neat, khaki uniform and sunglasses.

"Jeez, in trouble with the law already and I just got here." Maddy muttered under her breath and walked over to the car with hands held up in mock surrender. "Sorry, officer, I didn't know it was against the law to talk to your self here in Nielsen. Just arrived and got turned around."

"Yes, ma'am, I know. I know everyone hereabouts and you, as the saying goes, I'd remember." Looking her up and down with admiring deep blue eyes, he got out and motioned for her to put her hands down. A glint of recognition crossed his face.

"So? What did I do to deserve the flashing lights?" Maddy was too tired to be very deferential.

"If there's anything against the law here, I'd say it was having eyes the color of yours." He was flirting with her outrageously as he stared, the grin never faltering.

"Is that a cop-type compliment or just a typical come on?" Brazenly she folded her arms and leaned against the fender of his car.

She guessed he was at least six foot two of pure masculinity in a neat, tan uniform. Broad shoulders attached to muscular arms, neatly pressed uniform, a huge gun on his hip. This was a very attractive man and he hadn't even taken his sunglasses off. He walked around a bit, stretching his legs and leaned next to Maddy against the car. She looked away and wished her heart wouldn't flutter so.

The way she was feeling right now, there was nothing she

would love more than a good-natured exchange, especially with a handsome, if not rather smug, man. Pausing, she glanced back at her dusty car and ran a hand through her tousled red hair. Maddy readjusted the emerald green shirt that slid provocatively over her shoulder. She could see the interest in those brilliant blue eyes moving up and down her figure from the short skirt to the silky shirt constantly showing off a creamy shoulder.

Whoa, Girl. Let's not get anything started here we can't control. Just who was this guy, anyway? Why did he look so familiar?

"Well, ma'am, I was just making rounds when I saw you pull in. You looked a little lost," He said casually, readjusting his sunglasses.

"I am not lost, and it's miss." She said, "I was just getting my bearings. It's been a long time since I was here and I'm supposed to meet a realtor named Leland Lancaster." Maddy wished she didn't talk so fast, it made her sound nervous. The officer listened and seemed deep in thought.

"Yeah, his office is just down the street. Say, I know who you are now. I heard you might be coming in. So, is it really you?" He stood upright, grinning and apparently momentarily lost for words.

"Well, I know who I am, but who do you think I am?" Maddy knew she was being sassy, but she was tired and more than curious. Her heart lurched and uneasily she shifted from one foot to the other. Then the realization hit her. If this was who she thought it was, her stomach now joined her heart in bouncing like a ping-pong ball. Alec McKay. This was her first love. Well, that answered a lot of the questions she had. The first boy who ever kissed her, anyway, and the boy who never wrote to her? Well, maybe once or twice. That memory made her prickle.

"You still have the same habits, always on the move. And those big emerald green eyes never miss a thing. Nobody had eyes like you." He gently pushed a strand of her hair out of her eye. This time his voice was low and husky and made her heart flutter at the familiarity.

"I'm hardly the same girl. If you had bothered to write years ago, you might know me, at least a little. Too late now, I'm all grown up."

"I'll say you are." Deputy McKay took his glasses off and looked at her appraisingly.

Steadily his eyes locked on her. Something about the light hair, impish smile and knowing way he had about him when he looked at her made her feel fifteen again. His whole personality said teasing, sweet, sexy; and now all that in an adult version. It was him, and she did remember. "Well, this is a surprise," she said. *Now how was she going to handle it?* The deep blue of his eyes and the smile made her remember the honesty and trust they'd once shared. Could it still be that way or was he just trying to impress her?

I'm too suspicious, she chided herself, *give the guy a chance. Give yourself a chance..*

"Sorry, I was just thinking. Madeline Morris, haven't said that name in a long time. Junior High, I think. How many years has it been? I guess you could hardly be expected to remember me." He sounded hopeful rather than disappointed.

The big, brawny deputy stood before her holding his hands out in recognition as if expecting a hug.

As if she would ever forget that grin and the easy way

he smiled. But she wasn't going to admit it, not yet. She held her emotions in check.

"Oh, yes, I think— Oh, of course I remember you, Alec."

"Well, wouldn't expect you to remember me right off, I wasn't a great pen pal, was I?"

"I can't really remember." She shrugged.

"I remember I kissed you under the oak tree in front of the pavilion. Right over there, remember?" He pointed to a classic white bandstand that still stood in the middle of town.

"Yes, I remember. A girl always remembers her first kiss." She looked at his hand still holding hers. "Can I have my hand back?"

"Yes, but only if you let me make up all those years to you while you're here."

"I don't think so, not enough time. I'm not here for long."

He threw back his head, laughing a deep, tumultuous laugh that made her want to smile immediately at the sound. Then, unexpectedly, she found herself in a big hug, being twirled around. She struggled, surprised at how her heart still lurched around her long-distance, fickle, first love.

"For goodness sakes, put me down."

"Still the same little wild cat. And you do look and act like you did when we were kids. Maybe the hair is shorter. But I like short."

He finally let her go and stood back, hands on hips, a satisfied look on his face "Now that introductions are over, I have to say, you look great. That red hair, how I loved running my fingers through it, it was so soft and long."

Maddy was breathless from the hug as well as shock

of finding Alec seemingly as unchanged as when she last saw him.

"Well, I hardly know what to say to a greeting like that." She brushed non-existent dust from her clothes, trying to catch her breath from the exuberant welcome as well as her surprisingly excited response.

"You'll have to excuse me; I don't usually hug people I stop. But, you are a sight for sore eyes." He looked down at her, as if truly appreciative at her presence.

"So, you're a cop now. That's really ironic as ornery as you used to be to poor old Sheriff Maxwell when we were kids." Maddy, leaned against the car for support, hoping he didn't notice.

He waved her off. "We were angels compared to what I run into nowadays with these kids."

"Oh, so there is poetic justice after all." She couldn't hide the grin and he shrugged in sheepish agreement.

"I guess so. We were ornery, but we weren't dangerous." He stepped back and took another thoughtful look at her. "So, what are you doing back here in Nebraska?"

"My Aunt passed away."

"Oh, Maddy, I heard about your aunt. I'm so sorry."

Gently he put a hand gently on her forearm. "She was a great lady, always helping someone."

Surprised by his warmth and sympathy she stared back.

His touch was genuine, as true as his sensitive eyes, now darker and inquiring. There was nothing fake about this man. His caring was etched on his face as he looked intently at her.

"Maddy. I can't believe you're standing here. I hope things have been good for you."

"Good enough, I guess. Just look at you though."

"I know. Remember History class with Mrs. Warren? She never thought I'd amount to much, but I passed thanks to you. Still owe you for that." Maddy shrugged again and looked away.

"Hey, Maddy, I'm sorry about not writing much, losing touch. But, well, I tried to write. I did write a couple times. You got them, didn't you? I wasn't exactly a devoted writer, much less boyfriend, huh? I should have called more."

She looked away, not wanting him to know how much it had meant then.

"It was a long time ago, forget it. I only lived here six months, one semester. Life went on, for both of us. So, you're a cop now, and still in this one-horse town?"

"Oh but it's a two-horse town now, and yes, I love it here. Can't beat it. How about you? Married?"

"Married? Oh, no, at least not yet. My life is the usual. Went to school, got a job in Chicago. My parents are both gone now." She tried to sound casual, but his look said how sorry he was and her voice broke a little.

"I only wish I'd have known sooner about Aunt Madeline. When the letter came, well, I decided to come back myself. It's why I need to see this Leland Lancaster."

"I guess I forgot Miss Madeline was your kin. Sure I can't show you his office," he offered but she shook her head. It was time to put some space between him and the memories.

"Thanks. I'm sure I can find it from here, deputy." She hoped he noted the self-assurance more than the sadness in her voice. All these regrets were silly. It was water under the bridge. Looking at that face, hearing that laugh reminded her how important he had been to her once.

"Yes, I should get back on patrol, too. Can I call you Maddy? Better yet, can I just call you?"

Just like a scene out of a movie, and an old one at that. Maddy stood there thrilled but not sure if she should take the chance. *What is wrong with you, Girl?* Her instincts were at war with her self-pity after Larry's betrayal. Did that even matter now? She stared.

Deputy McKay gave her, urged her to take the chance. She didn't care, not when he looked at her like that.

His light hair was still short, wavy against deeply suntanned features with blue eyes that changed hues. Crinkle lines around his eyes from squinting in the sun only made him look more dashing.

"Alec, I'd better take your number since I don't know where I'm staying yet. I forgot my cell phone. This whole trip might have been for nothing. I mean, I don't know if I'll even be here very long. But thanks for the walk down memory lane. I'm glad I did get to see you again."

Flustered, she moved back from his lean, muscular body that seemed to draw her like a magnet. It had been way too long since she'd been held in his strong arms, or anyone's for that matter. What in the world was wrong with her, why was she fantasizing about a guy who hadn't bothered to keep in touch? Okay, so they were practically strangers now. But, one look at that big Cornhusker and her heart took off again.

His saucy grin was still lopsided as he wrote something on the back of a business card and handed it to her. "Here, my work number and cell are both on it."

She nodded but was thinking about that first kiss they shared as if it was yesterday. Alec had always been a big guy, he had to bend over just to kiss her. But he had grown into a handsome man, still in good shape. His uniform proved that as it fit tautly over his well-toned body.

She cleared her throat and nodded. "Okay, thanks. I'll call." She walked stiffly forward. How could she get so completely enamored by the mere sight of this guy?

It was a matter of trust, or lack of it. Larry Preston assumed he had control of her life, even throwing a ring her way thinking she'd jump at the chance. And now here came Deputy Sheriff Alec McKay who hadn't done anything to gain her trust, but then, he hadn't done anything to make her distrust him either. Except smile that earth-shattering smile, and look at her with those sexy dark blue eyes.

She paused and caught the deputy writing down her car plates in a small notebook.

"Very observant, deputy. I can see the streets of Nielsen will be safe tonight. But then, you always were quick to pick up the obvious." She teased and wagged a finger at him.

He walked slowly towards her with a sheepish grin.

"I'm sorry but I just had to see if your hair is as soft as I remembered." His finger touched the red-gold tresses, "and you used to wear it longer, down to here." He touched her chin and followed the line of her jaw until she slowly pulled away from his warm touch. "You said you hated that color because it always made you stand out in a crowd."

Amazingly he had done exactly what she had dreamed of him doing. "I said that?" Her soft breath teased his skin as if she'd kissed him. "If I did, I've changed my mind. I love the color. Do you?" Her hand rested on his chest and she could feel the muscles tighten at being so close. She hadn't meant to challenge him so soon. The feeling of being this close was her test and she was afraid she was about to fail.

"I've always loved this color. So, let's get together and

talk about it. Please, tell me this is only 'see you later' and not good by," he said with a voice that was low and seductive. He held her, as if refusing to release her until she agreed to meet later.

"Why, sheriff, am I irritating you?" she began, teasing him by using the wrong title again. His thumb rubbed her forearm gently and she couldn't hide the smile this time.

"My title is deputy, Maddy, and you know it. It's spelled d-e-p-u-t-y. D also stands for dope. I sure was one when I let you slip through my fingers. You'll call me, right? I need a chance to redeem my self for my lackluster writing skills. I will make it up to you if you'll let me."

"I'll call you, but I can't make any promises on how long I may be here until after I meet with Mr. Lancaster."

His hands loosened their grip in reply and gently moved up and down her arms as if it was the most natural thing in the world.

"I'll call later, deputy. After that we'll just have to see." Maddy wished she had her cell phone now. But, making him wait might be good. She smiled as he slowly drove by her on the street in his patrol car. Silently he drove beside her for a while before giving her a wave and speeding off. She just kept walking. A warm feeling surrounded her and her smile refused to fade. This was going to be an interesting trip after all.

The Lancaster Realty sign was partially hidden by landscaping and Maddy almost walked by it. Reaching for the door handle, she nearly collided with a large man in a stylish, grey pinstripe suit.

"I beg your pardon, Miss. May I help you?" The portly man with piercing dark eyes loomed over her. He wiped his brow with a large handkerchief, an expensive briefcase in the other hand. His black hair was tinged with gray and a neat mustache decorated his upper lip. He was quite a distinguished contrast to Deputy McKay.

What made her think such a thing? She needed to get her mind back to business at hand.

"If you're Leland Lancaster, you can. I'm Madeline Morris. I'm here about my great aunt's estate."

Mr. Lancaster's face registered surprise and he glanced at his watch. "It's nearly five Miss Morris, I wish you'd called."

"I did, Mr. Lancaster, a young lady said she'd tell you I'd be here this afternoon I am a bit late, however." Thanks to Deputy McKay, but she wasn't going to tell him that.

"She did? I didn't get any message. Oh, she did give me a note while I was on a conference call." He closed his eyes for a moment. "I'm sorry. Of course, you are Madeline O'Keefe's niece."

Maddy licked her lips and continued. "A Mr. Jack Drake wrote me and gave me your name." Fumbling in her purse she pulled out the formal looking letter. She couldn't help but feel she detected a brief shadow of uncertainty cross Mr. Lancaster's face when he heard her name.

The businessman rocked back on his heels, shaking his head. He grinned in embarrassment, or so Maddy thought. But then, her imagination seemed to be running overtime since her arrival in town.

"You were expecting me?"

"Oh, yes, I'm just surprised, is all. You got here so quickly. Yes, indeed. I am Leland Lancaster. Please, come in. It's just that I only notified Mr. Drake a few days ago. I found your name and address among some of your aunt's papers." Stepping back inside the office, Leland Lancaster flipped the lights on. The air conditioner rattled, but Maddy was grateful for the cool respite.

"My secretary is already gone for the day, but we can go in and discuss a few things. Get started on the paperwork and such. I'm sure you have questions."

Relieved, Maddy followed him into a neat office and watched as he closed the blinds hanging over the big plate glass window. A massive, old, oak desk gleamed in the fluorescent light, immediately catching her attention. The walls of the office were done in rich wood paneling.

"What a beautiful desk, Mr. Lancaster. It's from a very interesting period, and so well taken care of." Sliding her finger over the polished wood, she sat back in the leather chair he indicated.

"Well, thank you. Yes, it's an antique. I got it from a client of mind when he sold his estate at auction. You, ah, know your antiques."

"No, not really. I like antiques, is all. I read a lot in my line of work. I'm a librarian." She smiled and tried to relax. "I think I work with the written word so much I absorb things through my pores whether I know it or not." She laughed, but he didn't respond. So much for workplace humor, obvious that he missed the point altogether she thought to herself.

"Yes, I see. Now where in the world did that girl put the file? I don't know what Mr. Drake told you, but we're still looking for some papers your aunt misplaced. A dear, dear old lady, but not very organized, I'm afraid."

"I wouldn't know anything about that. I didn't know my great aunt very well. We only lived in Nielsen a short time when I was younger."

Looking around the office as Leland shuffled papers,

Maddy waited patiently while he went through files and other piles of paper.

"Oh, so you really didn't know her and her affairs and such? Your parents are both deceased, then?"

"Yes, killed in a car accident over two years ago. There are a few uncles and cousins left, but no one close to Great Aunt Madeline that I know of." Or, for herself for that matter, she thought sadly.

"I'm sorry to hear that. Part of the problem was in finding you. You were a very difficult young woman to locate." He smiled, wrinkling up his narrow nose. "Your great aunt married a man named O'Keefe. Madeline Morris O'Keefe. We found a marriage certificate and a death certificate, and various other papers saying he was an orphan and had no living relatives. Finally we found a letter with your parent's name and address. I let Mr. Drake, her lawyer, know that I'd found you and he contacted you from there."

"I hardly recall Great Aunt Madeline and I feel bad about that." Maddy spread her hands and then let them fall to her lap, a thousand questions on her mind.

"Well, she probably didn't know about your parents deaths. Miss Madeline was very old and had been ill a long time with cancer. You realize your parents were not named in the will, only you."

"Yes, that's what Mr. Drake's letter said. That's what I don't understand. There weren't any other friends or family members named?"

"No. None that we could find, like I said we had a heck of a time finding you. Evidently her husband died before she settled here, in the war, I believe. You may have not known her but she evidently knew all about you and wished you to have all her worldly possessions. We'll have to continue tomorrow, my secretary must have put the rest of the papers somewhere else. I can't seem to find what I want." He frowned at the stacks of paper now on his neat desk.

"Where are you staying so I can contact you in the morning?"

"Well, I had planned on a motel but they're booked solid clear back to the next town, I checked on my way here. I hate to think of driving around all night looking for a place. Would it be okay if I just stayed at my aunt's house tonight?" Maddy asked hopefully.

Leland rubbed his mustache, his eyes darted side to side, as if he were thinking of a reason to say 'no'. He wore a nice suit, but his tie was very loud colors in yellow and green. "I guess so."

"It would be a good place that's close. It's over 25 miles back to the turn off. I don't feel like driving that far tonight."

"Well, of course, the house is yours. Just the formality of reading the will is all. I'll get the key and I can accompany you over there. I just hope it's clean enough." He shrugged, loosening his ugly tie a bit.

"There's no need for you to bother going with me. I'm dead tired and could probably sleep on a picket fence, so this will do nicely."

"I can pick you up for breakfast at eight tomorrow morning. We'll get something to eat and get started on the paperwork."

"Make it nine at least, and you've got a deal."

"It's a date. Sure you don't want company going through the house for the first time?"

Maddy couldn't put her finger on it, but Leland Lancaster didn't appear too anxious for her to stay at the empty house.

Of course, she was so tired by this time that she didn't know what, if any motivation he had. Was it really concern for her safety and comfort? Or, was it something else?

Chapter 3

The streetlights flickered on in the soft dusk. Walking back to her car she noticed the crickets chirping and the quiet sounds of a small town winding down for the day.

"Careful, you could really get to like this type of living, Maddy," she said to herself, caught up in the freedom of walking alone at night. She loved to walk and run. Jogging opened her up, relaxed her from all the cares and stresses of the day. Some of her friends like to jog, but they weren't as devoted to it as she was. Rain or shine she picked her routes carefully in the big city, but here she felt she could be safe jogging by herself. This was a whole new world.

She found herself back at the house and her packed car. Grabbing two big bags from the trunk she proceeded up the sidewalk to her home. That realization hit her, too. She hadn't had a real home since her parents died.

As she stumbled up to the front door in the darkening, hot summer night, the house looked rather ominous. Thoughts of horror stories came back to haunt her steps. She was acting like a big baby.

Pausing at the bottom step, she shifted the heavy suitcases. How come it didn't affect her like this in the daytime? The trees seemed to moan softly as the soft, summer wind blew. The bushes scratched the long, narrow windows. This was silly, but she was definitely going to have those bushes trimmed. She placed her foot carefully on the first step, naturally the step creaked, and so did the next.

"Great. An hour ago it didn't look nearly so bad." Maddy said aloud, getting a firm grip on the heavy bags again. "I can't believe I said I'd stay here with or without lights." But she had. Chalk another one up to her big mouth. Always saying and doing things in the heat of the moment, just like her trip here.

"What's a city-bred, librarian doing in a place like this?" She wondered aloud with each successive step.

"That's exactly what I was thinking." The voice came from the depths of her worst nightmare and Maddy dropped her bags with a thud.

"For heaven's sake, deputy, you scared the wits out of me." Whirling, she found herself face-to-face with the Nielsen law again. Leaning weakly against the railing, she glared at Deputy McKay. "Is this what small town deputy's do, sneak up behind people? What are you, part Indian Scout or something? You nearly scared me to death."

"Gee, I don't believe so, if this gets out though, the bad buys might really start sweating it." Ignoring her disgruntled look, he crossed his arms over his chest and began fantasizing. "It'll go like this. The bad guys will be in the process of doing something illegal and, suddenly, there I'll be, right behind him."

"The old 'never knew what hit them' ploy, huh? Hope they have good health insurance." Regaining her composure, Maddy reached for the suitcases completely unnerved by the handsome man she was bantering with.

Deputy McKay took charge of the suitcases and motioned for her to proceed. "Come on, I just got off work and drove by hoping your meeting with Leland was over. How did it go?"

With the key in hand and Alec right behind her, the simple task of unlocking the door was even more difficult. His breath sent tingles up and down her spine and her hands were icy on the deadbolt lock. She motioned towards the house next door, nearly bumping heads.

Urging Maddy in, Deputy McKay brushed against her and she almost tripped, glaring at him in the dark.

"Your neighbor is Aunt Polly Smith. She's been looking out for you or the house. She was your aunt's best friend. You'll like her once you get to know her." The wind blew the door shut and Maddy jumped a foot.

"Scared of the bogeyman, Maddy?" His chuckle annoyed her, "I'll check the rooms, just in case."

"I'm not afraid of bogeymen, deputy. I'll have you know I've lived in the big city long enough on my own." Maddy stepped around gingerly in the dark looking for Deputy McKay. She listened as his steps faded away, berating herself for having such a wild imagination.

"Yeah, it sure looked like it. You were shaking in your boots when I came up, staring at the big, bad, spooky house."

Alec's voice echoed in the back of the house gleefully. "If I remember right, you were a scaredy-cat back in junior high too," his teasing laugher echoed back at her.

"I was not. Not then or now. The luggage was heavy and, I couldn't find my key." Why didn't she just be quiet, every word sounded even more childish than the last.

"Oh, yeah, remember when we all went out to the Pioneer grave? Everyone jumped the creek and you wouldn't even get out of the car. Let's see, what was the curse? If you touched the gravestone, you'd die within a year."

"Looking back on it now that was so immature. I worried about everyone who touched it for months. But I haven't thought of that in ages. Can we please drop it and get back to the matter at hand? I have a flashlight in the car. Mr. Lancaster said he wasn't sure about the utilities." The lights snapped on suddenly, catching her by surprise. Pointing to the overhead light Deputy McKay leaned next to the wall switch.

"And then there was light. I aim to please." The shock of having the lights on came as a great relief, even if Alec stood there smirking. She noticed something different about him rather than the house just then. Instead of his uniform he'd changed into snug, washed-off blue jeans, a black Cornhusker tee shirt that stretched over his muscular chest and arms, and comfortable running shoes. He looked very casual and sexy.

They stood in the little entryway. A big, mirrored hat rack that served as a chair, umbrella stand and plant table guarded the front door, obviously an antique. A long hall led back to the kitchen and some other rooms.

A telephone desk with an old black dial phone sat near

the stairway. Long, Persian throw rugs covered the wood floors, double sliding doors stood behind the cocky deputy. Grandly stepping back he opened them with a flourish of his arm, revealing a small library or den.

"You're no Vanna White, deputy," Maddy said as she brushed past him, "It's so lovely, so elegant. The bedrooms are upstairs if I remember right." She didn't realize Deputy McKay was hot on her heels again.

"I think so. Want to go check them out?" His wink was wicked with insinuation. Her frown didn't deter his teasing, or from him following her into the big, dark living room to the left of the stairs.

"Thanks, but I'll pass. What's this? Everything's covered in sheets."

"Maid's night out, I guess." Alec looked around, partly interested and always professional. "I haven't been inside for ages. It's been closed up since she went into the nursing home."

"I'm so glad the electricity is on." Having light was having a little control of the situation.

"Guess Leland should have paid more attention. I saw him here just last week. Hey, I bet the gas and water are on, too." He walked back into the kitchen.

"Leland checked in here just last week, you say? Then why did he say the utilities had been cut off?" Alec evidently didn't hear her and she shrugged, too tired to care. Maybe the realtor just forgot, but it seemed strange.

Maddy pulled several sheets off a couch and some chairs while she heard Alec puttering around in the kitchen. He returned with a satisfied look on his face.

"Good news, gas and water are both on, and what's

more important, no bogeymen." He held up his hands in a scary pose.

"You're not going to let that one die, are you? Thanks, sheriff." Maddy teased him back.

Scrunching his eyebrows together in mock frustration he replied patiently, "That's deputy sheriff, and all kidding aside, if you need anything, I hope you call me. The number is by the phone. Oh, that's working, too, even though it's old. You have my card. But tell me this, are we still friends?"

He held out his hand and she paused only a moment before taking it. He had an innately captivating presence.

The firm grip captured more than her hand, her heart seemed to flutter again.

"I admit I'd like that, Alec. I still don't know how long I'm going to be here, but a girl can't have too many friends. I'll just bet you have the girls in town lined up waiting on you. I wouldn't want to horn in or anything." Maddy gently extracted her hand and eyes from his.

He threw her a well-polished look and shook his head "No, they all know me too well."

"I'll bet. Say, how did you know I'd be coming back here to the house? Don't tell me you waited? Did you wait for me to come back?" She didn't know whether to be flattered or irritated.

"Oh, that. Well, it has to do with your nosy neighbor, Mrs. Smith. She's like a one-woman neighborhood watch. You were right about having a witness. She called me tonight about you. She was worried about prowlers again."

"There have been prowlers here before?" Maddy rubbed her arms uneasily.

Deputy McKay brightened as if with a sudden idea.

"Say, if you're uneasy about staying here alone, I'm free." He began but she interrupted him. He was a little too eager.

"Thanks, but, I'll manage."

"Well, if you change your mind. Oh, and as for the prowlers, it was probably just some kids goofing off but maybe it's not a good idea for you to stay here alone."

"Yes, probably," she said weakly, "but I am, so quit trying to convince me to leave. I'm beat and I'm still puzzled why Leland didn't tell me about any of this."

Alec shrugged, looking around. He pulled a well-worn Nebraska baseball cap out of his back pocket and put it on, his eyes glinted in the reflection of the mirror above the fireplace.

"It sure is a nice house."

"Did you know my aunt very well?"

"Everyone in town knew Miss Madeline. She was a classy lady, always helping someone. I felt bad when she got sick, didn't see her much after that." He was looking around absently. "Don't you know your own relatives?"

"Not really. She was my father's aunt, I'm named for her but we were here such a short time. Don't you remember when we left? It was awful. I didn't want to leave but it's strange. Since I've arrived, I sometimes feel a connection just being here around her things. My great grandmother hated Aunt Madeline for some reason, and the rest of the family was all so scared of her they never spoke of Aunt Madeline except to call her the Black Sheep of the family. All but my father, he loved her."

"Sounds like something Miss Madeline would have planned. She was really smart, very creative."

The pensive sound of his voice was gentle, caressing. "You said something about a boyfriend before, is it serious?"

Maddy flushed and ignored his question. Feigning interest she picked up some of the knickknacks sitting around her aunt's living room. Apparently everything was just as she left it. It suddenly dawned on Maddy she'd confided a lot of personal things to Alec just now. It amazed her she did that, even if he had been, or, was, a friend. If there ever was a time she needed someone to talk to, it was now. But could she trust him?

"I would rather not talk about that any more. Are you off-duty now?" Maddy changed the subject, fingering heavy satin tassels that tied back velvet curtains framing the archway to the living room. Deputy McKay's blue eyes didn't miss anything and he nodded.

"Yes, on my way home when Aunt Polly caught up to me. So, thought I'd be neighborly and drop by. I explained the situation with you and the house to her, too."

"You know, you take after your aunt some. I think it's the red hair maybe, or the eyes. But it's there." He made a frame with his fingers like a photographer, head cocked at an angle as he toyed with her heart. The grin slowly faded as his breath came out a little ragged. Rubbing his chin, he stepped back as if breaking a spell, the impish grin returning.

"You know, I'm beginning to remember more and more about you, about us, and that semester at school. You sure, you don't want me to stick around for a while?" His eyes were playing tricks on hers, his voice hopeful as if wishing she'd change her mind.

Did he remember their first kiss, too, she thought. It had been so special, tender. They had waxed poetic about it then.

Later, they'd made teenaged promises, sharing plans, goals. Suddenly she snapped back.

"I sure hope there are some pictures of my aunt around somewhere," Maddy changed the subject once again, avoiding the magnetism that seemed to draw her to him. "I feel like I missed out on so much, but I want to catch up while I'm here."

"There'll be plenty of time to catch up on her life. Now, getting back to us, we were pretty serious about each other. Didn't we go to a dance together that year?" Alec cleared his throat, amusement flickered in his eyes.

Shrugging, she couldn't look at him. She had been very serious. They spent every moment together and had gone to the homecoming dance that year. She looked over at him standing so casually in the doorway. Was he thinking like she was, remembering? They'd gone for a long walk, kissed under the oak tree in the square. It was her first kiss. He'd even carved their initials on the bandstand, against town regulations. Did he remember all that? She did. But she said nothing because it evidently didn't mean as much to him as it had to her.

"I wish I had known her better. Maybe I could have helped."

"If it's any consolation, she had a lot of good friends around her. The whole town helped. The women brought in food and cleaned. The men cut the grass in summer, scooped snow in winter. We kept it up until she had to go to the nursing home. Now Aunt Polly is the only one who keeps tabs on the place, done a good job, too. She is your suspicious neighbor. She'll be glad to meet you, like me."

He raised his brows and gave her a wink. The look

spoke volumes and Maddy was torn between excitement and caution at the flirtation. She opened her mouth to speak but nothing came out. How could she answer that?

"So, are you are going to stick around at least for a while?"

"I will for a while. Don't know how long yet. I hadn't planned on it permanently, I've got a job, you know." Anonymous sounding words came out of her mouth, not very convincing but at least it was something.

He stepped ahead quickly cutting off her exit, his strong arm blocking the doorway. "You really like that job, I mean you wouldn't even consider staying a while? You might get to like it here." His breath was soft on her cheek. She could smell the faint aroma of his aftershave, all woodsy and clean.

"My job is my job. Of course I like it. What kind of a question is that?" She felt cornered.

"I'm sorry. I guess I'm getting ahead of myself. It's just that I feel like I'm getting a second chance at something important here and you mentioned a boyfriend. I don't mean to pry but you didn't sound very happy about it. Like I said if you ever need someone to talk to, I'm available."

It was hard to admit she'd left behind a dead-end job, a lonely apartment, and a boyfriend she didn't trust. True she had friends and felt comfortable in her little apartment, but only because it was convenient. The scary part was she had been tempted to go back just because she didn't want to face the thought of change. But she'd be darned if she would admit that to herself, or him, now.

"To tell you the truth, Alec, I'd planned to dispose of my great aunt's things as quickly as possible. After all, I had no reason to think there was anything for me here. It's a pretty small town after living in Chicago. I don't think I'm much of a small town girl. I don't know if I'd be content here."

"Well, that makes sense, I guess." Alec regarded her quizzically for a moment, but if he was disappointed, he didn't say so. It made her feel awful inside, but stubbornly she fought it off, wanting some breathing room.

"I have a full life back in Chicago. I can't, just, up and, well, you know, leave." She struggled again.

He shrugged, this time when he looked at her it was in a different light.

"I pushed too hard, you don't need to explain anything to me. It's just been good seeing you, really, Maddy." He smiled and excused himself. "Hey, I'll go check the back door and make sure everything is locked up for the night and then I better get going. I've got an early shift in the morning."

Maddy only half noticed his departure. Her head was throbbing equally from fatigue and stress. She hadn't planned on sparring with Alec. She hadn't expected him to even be in Nielsen anymore. But how could he presume to interfere in her life? If only he'd kept in touch all those years ago, just a few lousy letters might have made all the difference in her life.

Stepping cautiously into the living room, she gazed in wonder at the room so lovingly arranged. Even under sheets and in a dusty state, the room flowed in beauty with rich wood and classic, elegant taste. Slowly she uncovered a few more pieces, running her hand over the mantle of the old fireplace, long unlit. Her feet sank into the plush, delicately flowered carpet.

Emotion overwhelmed her, envisioning her great aunt greeting guests in the ambiance of this very room. Gently

Maddy touched the velvet fainting couch and pulled the sheet from the ornate settee. Cleverly arranged knick-knacks, little music boxes, southern belles dancing on porcelain pedestals, birds in ceramic branches sat as they had when Aunt Madeline had lived here.

The mirror above the fireplace showed her reflection, the wonder of living such a life. Suddenly a man's strong features appeared beside her, Alec. They looked at each other through the mirror's eyes.

His hand rested gently on her shoulder and Maddy yearned to lean back into his arms, wondering if it could be the way she remembered it after so many years. It would be easy to do, but would it be right?

Remembering the way she was then, the way she felt drawn to this little town, her feelings now being turned inside out. Meeting him was coincidence? How did she fall under his trance, this handsome, impulsive, deputy. It could turn out to be an improbable situation.

"There are a few things in the freezer and coffee in the cupboard for breakfast. That is, unless you'd care to have breakfast with me." His voice was oddly gentle.

Maddy swallowed hard trying not to smile at his invitation "How nice of you to ask me, but Mr. Lancaster insisted we meet for breakfast, get an early start on the paperwork and all. You understand?"

"I can't believe you are going out with a guy twice my age." He shook his head and grinned at her teasingly. "It's just my luck to be beaten to the punch by him."

If the truth be known, she would have much rather gone to eat with Alec than her aunt's rather strange realtor, but she wasn't going to let him know that.

"I have to get this estate paperwork wrapped up. Sorry." She really was contrite.

"You could cancel and reschedule with your Mr. Lancaster." Alec said coyly.

"He's not *my* Mr. Lancaster, and why in the world would you say something like that? He's been completely professional from what I can tell." Maddy crossed her arms a bit defensively.

"I wish you would tell me what's really bothering you instead of hiding behind this murky suspicion. I know you're a cop and all, I mean a deputy sheriff, sorry. But if there's something I should know, I wish you'd just spit it out."

"No, no, nothing like that. Just my cop instincts flaring, I guess."

"I see. Well, I appreciate the concern when it comes to prowlers anyway. Glad you decided to hang around. But I'm perfectly capable of taking care of myself."

"I'm sure you are but I'm glad I hung around here too. I'm very glad you decided to make the trip back yourself, Maddy." His larger hand engulfed hers. A vaguely sensuous feeling passed between them. "Very glad," he repeated and squeezed her hand gently as he turned to go.

"I still think you should have breakfast with me and meet Leland later, but, your decision." He lifted his hand in a wave as he went down the steps.

Maddy watched him saunter down the sidewalk. The emotional weight of the day had worn her down to a nub. She couldn't help but smile at meeting Alec and the memories she held in her heart like reality once again. It just surprised her how strongly she felt about them and him.

"Take care, deputy. Maybe I'll see you tomorrow. Sorry

Leland beat you to the draw for breakfast." She smiled and waved back.

She still had a subtle feeling that she was a stranger coming in and taking over. What if people thought she was just here for what she could get? Is that how it always looked during inheritances? Maybe that's why she felt guilty. It's what she had thought she would do herself at first.

The doorbell rang just then and thinking it was Alec come back for another sparring match, she yanked the door open. "If you've come back to argue, I'm not in the mood. Oh, my goodness. I'm sorry. I thought you were someone else. You're the neighbor, next door. Hi, come in."

A bewildered looking older woman with a tin foil covered plate in her hand stood at the door.

"Have I come at a bad time, my Dear?" Peering over her glasses she sighed, "I have come at a bad time. You don't even know me and here I stand so late in the evening. What did Alec say about me? Said I was snoopy, didn't he?"

"Yes, I mean, no, he merely said we were neighbors. I'm Maddy Morris. Alec and I seemed to disagree about the impression one makes on other people sometimes."

"Well, according to him you haven't seen each other for fifteen years. That's a long time. You need to go slow."

"I see he's been talking to you already. Well, I agree, and I think he does too, now, Mrs. Smith."

"Good. You two have plenty of time to catch up." Aunt Polly handed her the dish and looked Maddy up and down carefully. "You can call me Aunt Polly like everyone else in town. That's coffeecake for breakfast, by the way." She patted Maddy's hand, a friendly bond forming between the two women instantly.

"My, my, you do favor her. Your aunt, Miss Madeline, I mean."

"I do? It's strange to hear that, but nice. I'd like to hear more about her and her life here sometime if you don't mind, that is." Maddy was intrigued.

"One thing you'll learn about me, my dear, is I like to talk. I'd love to acquaint you with her, after the fact, of course. Such a shame she's gone, I miss her a lot. Alec said you didn't remember her."

"He has been talking a lot. Well, I guess it's no secret. I was in junior high the last time I saw her. To be truthful, I don't think I paid much attention when I was here. Just being a stupid kid."

"Not stupid, just being a kid." Aunt Polly said graciously.

Maddy went into the kitchen with Aunt Polly following behind. "I think Alec's feelings are hurt because Leland asked me out to breakfast in the morning." Maddy said carefully. "He didn't say anything but I think he was disappointed."

"I see. Well, people in Chicago do eat breakfast don't they?" Her quizzical look revived Maddy's humor.

"Yes, even we eat breakfast in Chicago, Aunt Polly. What the good deputy objects to, is who I'm having it with."

"Oh, I'm not surprised." The older woman nodded. "I don't think that's much of his business, do you?"

"Exactly, but I didn't say it that way." Maddy felt vindicated.

"There'll be plenty of time for you two to go out later."

Maddy swallowed hard. "I don't think I'll be here long enough for that distinct pleasure. But I'm sure there must be a lot of women wanting to go out with Alec."

Aunt Polly looked pensive but didn't speak.

"Well, it's awfully late, my dear. I wanted to apologize for staring at you this afternoon when you arrived. My eyes aren't as good as they once were, but you know I think Alec is right, you do look a lot like your aunt."

"Thank you, that makes me feel very good. I'm a little low on relatives at the moment, the few I have I don't like much." Maddy walked to the front door with her.

"Well, she knew you and loved you, young lady. I can tell you that, and more. But, it's getting late. I thought I'd drop by when I saw Alec's patrol car out front. See if you needed anything."

"By the way, Alec and Leland Lancaster don't always get on but don't let it bother you. Don't know why exactly. He's done some work for me and gets a little full of himself, irritates me sometimes too, but, we enjoy getting on each other's nerves. I think you just need to keep an eye on him." Aunt Polly finished with a knowing look. "I understand Alec's reaction." She chuckled under her breath.

"You don't know why?" Maddy wondered.

"Not really, just the way Leland does things. A lot of us don't see eye to eye with him. So, are you going to be okay?"

"I'm fine. I just need a place to rest my head tonight and then tomorrow I hope to know more about things."

"Seems like Alec wants to catch up where you two left off." Aunt Polly said knowingly glancing into the living room as they passed it.

Her new friend and neighbor waved a wrinkled hand and laughed. "Oh, he's got more virtues than vices. I imagine you'll find that out. Besides, there's plenty of time. One thing, though, your great aunt thought a great deal of your parents and you. Bless her soul. I still miss her."

"I miss her and I hardly knew her." Maddy said sadly.

"I just know Madeline told me she didn't ever want anyone from the old days to know where she was. Only kept in touch with your folks and they promised not to tell. Funny about the past, 'It'll all come out one day,' she used to say to me, 'when it's time.'"

Aunt Polly shrugged and stepped out in the cool, summer evening. She wiped her eyes with a white handkerchief. "She had her reasons and I respected them. Maybe it's time now for it to all to be laid to rest."

Maddy leaned on the door, exhausted, suddenly overwhelmed by everything. "I hope so. Okay then, all in good time, Aunt Polly, good night."

"I still can't get over Alec," The spry little old lady with appropriately enough round granny glasses and spiffy white Reeboks on, chuckled as she went down the walk. "He let Leland beat him asking you out. He's got a good heart though, Honey. Good night.

"Good night, Aunt Polly. Thanks for the coffee cake." Maddy still felt conflicted.

"Give me a call when you get back from breakfast. Mind you, watch that Leland, like I said. Don't let him talk you into signing anything until you sleep on it. It's best to keep your wits about you."

Maddy would have loved to ask why they both warned her about Leland Lancaster. This Leland didn't appear to be a ladies man, and they couldn't say anything bad about him, but one could never tell. Locking the door securely, she flipped off the outside lights, leaning wearily on the banister. She would just make sure she watched everything closely. What an odd assortment of people she had met this day.

Eyeing the phone, she thought about calling Chicago to let her friends know she had arrived safely but she wasn't in any mood to hear their list of concerns. Later the last thought skittering across her mind as she pulled the hand made quilt up to her chin consisted of wavy, light hair and big blue eyes staring at her. It had been a long time since she went to sleep dreaming about a man.

"Good night, Deputy Sheriff Alec McKay, wherever you are. I think it might prove interesting to stay around for at least a little while, just to find out what makes you tick," Maddy said yawning widely. Seconds later the soft feather pillow cushioned her into a dream world full of new thoughts and old memories.

Chapter 4

Jerking awake early the next morning, Maddy couldn't figure out why she felt so exhausted. Until she recalled dreaming all night of her and Leland and Alec in a boxing ring. The thought of sparring in person with either of them wasn't any more appealing now. *Darn men.* Plumping up the pillows, she sat back and looked around the room. She felt surrounded by her great aunt's personality as well as her personal possessions.

Delicate, pale yellow wallpaper with small roses covered the walls. Very feminine. The open window allowed a gentle breeze to billow the filmy, sheer curtains in and out. She loved her aunt's taste even if it was old fashioned. If she hadn't worried that Leland Lancaster might catch her in bed, she would have pulled the covers up and gone back to sleep.

The solid, old, four-poster bed was comfortable. The massive bedposts stood slightly higher than her waist, thick, round and smooth. A tall dresser and dressing table with stool and mirror matching the bed stood in alignment. A small, delicate woman's writing desk sat next to the window.

Her frustration was mostly Deputy Alec McKay's fault. Maddy realized she'd let what that darn deputy think influence her, even when she didn't realize it. He had a lot of nerve. After letting people boss her for so long, she was not going to put up with it anymore. When she got home from this meeting she knew what she wanted to do. Explain a few things to a certain deputy sheriff. She'd do it quickly and then head back to Chicago and away from this know-it-all who thought he could charm her with his handsome face and sexy smile. Yes, that's just what she would do.

"There better be enough hot water for a shower after all this." She was pleased to find there weren't any problems with the hot water heater.

The bathroom had been remodeled into a rather large, lavish bath with space enough for a comfortable chair and small armoire chest full of towels. An old, claw-footed bathtub stood at the far end, with, thank goodness, a showerhead.

At quarter to nine, Maddy emerged wearing a flattering navy blue sundress and matching spectator pumps. She wanted to look especially sophisticated and professional just in case Leland Lancaster did try and take advantage of her. She'd be ready

While wandering around inside waiting for Leland, Maddy pulled several more sheets from the lovely antiques and found a small, portable TV which she wheeled into the kitchen and turned on. A voice in the big, empty house made the surroundings more homey.

There were a few things to eat in the freezer, dried goods in the pantry, a well-stocked laundry room in back. No more Laundromats came to her mind. The thought of all the clothes in those awful machines that had eaten or been shrunk into nothingness back home made her feel victorious, at least momentarily.

That was the most practical solution. Sell everything, pay the bills, and get her car out of hock and the dentist off her back and then what?

"Come on, Leland. Let's get this show on the road already." She knew she was okay when she began talking to herself. The thinking was getting to her. Snapping off the TV, Maddy went outside to wait. It was a beautiful day. Hands clasped behind her, she walked slowly around the house looking at the grounds.

Mentally Maddy found herself reseeding here and re-caulking there. The challenge excited her more than she had thought anything could again. Perhaps, just, perhaps but a toot of a car horn interrupted her thoughts.

Leland Lancaster drove a big car so white it almost hurt her eyes. He and the car were a fine match, both were overpowering. This morning he wore a tan suit and light blue shirt.

"Well, Miss Morris. Good morning. Did you sleep well in that old house last night?" Not giving her a chance to answer he continued, "I'm sure it's nothing compared to what you are used to in Chicago. Small town living is quite different from the big city, huh? I'm sure we can get things settled quickly enough and you can get back to your life, with a nice inheritance to help you along."

His attitude irritated Maddy. But he was right.

"The house was anything but drafty. Mrs. Smith from next door has been keeping things up nicely." She looked him squarely in the eye. "Luckily I had visitors last night to welcome me to town. I was just fine there."

"You had visitors? Last night?" Leland Lancaster frowned and gave a shrug, "Imagine that. I bet I know, Aunt Polly for one, am I right? That deputy sheriff probably showed up too. Anything you want to know, ask Aunt Polly. Oh, I mean that in the kindest way, of course."

"Deputy McKay and I are old schoolmates. They were kind enough to check in on me. I guess since I'm alone and everything. Oh, and by the way," watching for his reaction she added, "the utilities were all on. Someone had to be paying the bills to have them on this long."

Without missing a step, he shrugged and said, "Well, yes, I see, that's one of the things I want to discuss with you this morning. It seems we have been keeping the utilities up, authorized through your aunt's attorney, of course. My secretary forgot to tell me, but she has been taking care of it. We'll get into all that later."

"Just when do I get to meet this, Mr. Drake?"

"He was in court this morning in Omaha, but, I'm sure he'll make a trip out here today. He said he'd call."

Maddy climbed in and sat back in the plush passenger seat and smiled confidently. He better believe they'd get into all of this. Mr. Lancaster looked cool and calm this morning as he drove down the street, chatting with Maddy.

"I hope that old Mrs. Smith didn't bother you too much, she can be such a busybody sometimes. That deputy too, he's forever interfering, calling about every little thing. Trying to be helpful I'm sure, but a bother all the same."

"No, everyone's been very kind. I'm finding Nielsen a very friendly town. In fact, it hasn't changed much since I lived here. A little more modernized, but still a very charming and friendly town."

The small town bustled with activity with people going about their business as they drove down the main street.

"That's nice of you to say, Miss Morris. We all like to think our town is special, friendly. Nice place to visit after a long absence, how long has it been?"

"A long time, I was fourteen or fifteen, I think." Maddy said absently.

"I hope you won't think me presumptuous to give a little friendly word of warning. I mean, you being away for so long, a lot of things do change. People, for instance. You think you know them, but you really don't."

"I suppose that true sometimes." She stared at him.

"Well, you're an attractive young woman with a wonderful personality, and, I'm sure you'll be quite well off after the estate is settled. You must be careful, you know, a young woman with a lot of money is temping to some people. Do you have someone to advise you?"

Maddy paused, not sure how much she wanted to share about her business. "Yes, back in Chicago. Don't worry. I'm not an impulsive type, Mr. Lancaster. No Las Vegas trips for me."

"You didn't strike me as the impulsive type, Miss Morris, but never hurts to be careful."

"Well, thank you for the warning, Mr. Lancaster. But, after living in the city, being mugged twice and burglarized three times, I think I can handle myself or, anyone else for that matter."

"Well, just trying to help. I know it must be difficult coming back to town after so long." He said in a businesslike manner. "All part of my service. Mr. Drake and I have been taking care of your aunt's interests for a while and I just thought I should warn you. Knowing your dear aunt the way I did, she'd have wanted me to look out for you."

The temptation to repeat the warnings she'd had about him was hard to resist, but just then they pulled into a large, neat-looking truck stop, and the conversation ended.

"Not much atmosphere but the food is good and we can hear ourselves think without noise and interruption." Leland declared, pulling his massive car in an empty space. Eager to get things going Maddy nodded and followed him in.

Leland hurried to open the door and escort her in. Maddy took note, he was polite. The big neon sign read, "Truckers Heaven" and along with several big rigs and a bevy of pick ups, sat one, lone, deputy sheriff's patrol car.

"Who would have thought," Maddy muttered to herself. "On your toes, girl."

"Morning, Leland. Hi, Miss." A pretty, black-haired waitress greeted them, grabbing menus and a coffee pot, and showing them to a back table. Maddy's heels clicked on the clean, tile floor and she noticed the group of men just about the same time they noticed her.

"Welcome to Nielsen, Miss." The waitress's nametag read "Dixie" and her smile was genuine. "Say, Honey, I hear you're related to Miss Madeline. She was a really, fine lady. We sure miss her."

"I see the town gossips didn't waste any time spreading the news about your arrival." Leland sighed, "Sometimes small towns can be a bit intrusive."

"I think it's nice that everyone loved my great aunt so much."

"Well, it is small town living at its best." He agreed. They ordered a couple of specials with coffee and Maddy soon caught Deputy McKay staring and waved, giving a little salute. His smile was dazzling and made her smile back even though Leland frowned.

With a slight nod, she pretended to listen to Leland while watching the other men at the deputy's table. They straddled chairs or stood casually about, laughing and talking, looking over at her and smiling broadly. Wishing she could hear their conversation it had to be more interesting than the information Leland was dutifully giving her about the town and her inheritance in general. He was serious and she turned her attention back to the realtor.

He seemed well versed in real estate and determined to give her thorough, well-rounded approach to her situation.

"Here you go, Miss Morris, a large orange juice." Dixie sat a huge glass in front of her. Maddy hadn't ordered orange juice and looked up, puzzled.

"Oh, it's courtesy of Deputy McKay, over there."

They all glanced over and the deputy raised his juice glass in a salute. "Yeah, he said you city girls need lots of Vitamin C, something about smog and such." Dixie patted Maddy's arm, "He's just funning with you, he's a real sweetheart." Leland shook his head and sighed at the interruption.

"Yes, tell him thank you for me. He keeps saying how wonderful small town life is. I'm beginning to believe him." She held up her glass when he looked over at her and took a big sip.

"That deputy is really something. He seems to forget his

job and always flirting with the girls. Sometimes I wonder if he's fit to wear the uniform," he fumed.

Things settled down after that and they finished their meal in peace. What Leland Lancaster didn't know was she had gone through the same thing with her parent's estate. Granted, it wasn't as big as this one, but she knew the ups and downs of settling an estate. Maddy knew what she needed to do.

"Now, if you wish I can dispense with any further bothersome paperwork, just sign these papers and I'll take care of everything for you. You can go back to Chicago and I'll just call or email everything to you."

He sounded like Larry Preston, so self-assured and smug she had trouble not laughing in his face. Leland Lancaster thought he had most likely pulled one off on the new kid in town. Maybe he did it innocently, maybe not. Maddy thought it was what both Alec and Aunt Polly warned her about, not really dishonest but close to it.

"Well, that would be okay, except I want to read everything thoroughly, first, Mr. Lancaster." She reached for the papers, brushing aside the outstretched hand holding his ink pen. She glanced at the papers, tapped them straight and put them beside her purse.

He cleared his throat. "Oh, of course, that is a good idea. However, I merely was trying to save you time and money. I thought you wanted to get back to Chicago, your job and all." His inference puzzled her. She'd never mentioned anything of the sort to him.

"I appreciate your concern, Mr. Lancaster but I'll wait to meet with Mr. Drake." Looking intently at him, Maddy sat back with a deliberate air of confidence, "You know things may change. I may just decide to stay. I find Nielsen a very nice town."

She could see it was a comment he wasn't anticipating. "Stay? You mean, here in Nielsen? What in the world would you do that for? It'd be a welcome addition, I must say, but a puzzle."

"Well, when I woke up in the house this morning, I don't know, something just felt right about it. I guess you just can never tell about some people." Maddy replied glibly, sheer coincidence that her eyes came to rest on Alec McKay, chewing a soda straw and gazing back at her thoughtfully. "And to tell you the truth, I've thought the house might do well as a bed and breakfast inn. It's just a thought, but there's enough room."

"Well, you certainly have been thinking about things, haven't you? It's entirely up to you, but, I would advise you to move slowly. No one's lived in it for a while. It might need more renovation for a plan like that. In any case, we better get back to the office, Miss Morris."

Another big laugh came floating across the room from the deputy and his friends. So, while Maddy waited for Leland to pay the bill, she decided to beard the lion in his den and casually sauntered over. If she could handle Leland, she thought she could handle Alec.

"Thanks again for the orange juice. I feel invigorated, Deputy McKay." Clutching her purse under her arm, Maddy approached the table full of men. She looked at them, seeing an assortment of shapes and sizes.

"Good morning, gentlemen." A nod to them all caused a brief silence then suddenly the table erupted with warm greetings.

A bushy-bearded man with a *GO BIG RED* cap and deeply tanned complexion spoke first.

"Now Miss, you got to tell me why you'd sit over there with old Leland when you could have been at a table of good old boys like us?" He snapped suspenders that were pulled taut over an ample beer belly. "Our fearless lawman would have been right here to protect you or," and he winked, "we would have been here to protect you from him, since he's been paying more attention to your table than ours since you got here."

Maddy kept her sense of humor, glancing at Leland who waited impatiently to pay his bill behind several truckers.

"I just came over to thank the good deputy for the orange juice. A lot of oranges had to die to fill that glass." Laughter from all around the table filled the air. "It was, to say the least, a little more than I'm used to, but then," she walked behind the deputy's chair and trailed her finger over the back of it, demurely, "there's a lot of things around here that are more than I'm used to." The bearded man laughed gleefully, slapping Alec on the shoulder with a resounding thump.

"Now, a fellow could take that one of two ways, Miss Morris," Deputy McKay sat forward and rubbed his shoulder.

"I'm afraid you'll have to take it any way you want, deputy. I'm just a poor, little city girl, learning the ways of the country. And who are these handsome gentlemen?"

Alec reluctantly introduced everyone around the table of eight men. "I'm probably cutting my own throat introducing you to these bums," he said good naturedly. "When my back is turned some of them will be asking you for a date, Maddy."

"Well, since we're just old school friends, that shouldn't upset you."

"Yes, it's true. We went to school here together." Alec held up his hands, grinning impishly at her and finished with a bow.

"Hello. It's nice to meet everyone. Please, call me Maddy. Except you." All eyes fell on the deputy, "You can call me Miss Morris."

Everyone laughed as Alec had to accept the teasing but he finally shook his head and smiled, "We'll talk about that later, Miss Morris."

"Gee, deputy, a girl could take that one of two ways." Maddy arched her eyebrows and gave a challenging grin.

Leland had paid the bill and was now hurrying over to her so she said good by and joined the realtor at the door.

The rest of the morning was spent going over papers with Leland and Jack Drake who showed up after lunch. The actual will was brief and simple enough. Her great aunt had left everything she owned to Maddy. But Leland seemed determined to stretch things out as if it were more difficult. Jack Drake, the attorney didn't help much, arriving an hour late as Leland hemmed and hawed his way through endless paperwork.

Mr. Drake was older than she'd thought, tall, slim and white haired, in his late 60s, Maddy guessed. Leland was very pleased to see him and they acted like old friends. It was obvious he admired the Omaha attorney and never missed a chance to emphasize his own achievements to the older man. Together they appeared like a professional team. Mr. Drake's grip was firm, and he appeared impressed when Maddy didn't back down from his impervious stare when they were introduced.

Being left the house didn't surprise Maddy. Further

discussion included Mr. Drake handing over a healthy checking account, a savings account and a rather ambiguous entry concerning 'Miscellaneous Bonds' that were all hers. Maddy was speechless for a moment before recovering enough to let her business sense take over.

"What are these 'Miscellaneous Bonds'," she asked point blank. The men exchanged looks.

"That's what we're attempting to find out." Jack Drake started to pack his briefcase and Leland nodded in agreement. "I'm relatively certain the bonds are worthless, if it's the ones that I remember her telling me about."

"They are in the name of the C.G. Johnson Mining Company and we can't find the actual bonds anywhere. By that, I mean your aunt probably misplaced or threw the bonds away because they weren't worth anything. Leland and I briefly searched for them before you arrived but couldn't locate them. We didn't go through the house, just her desk in the library. Have you come across anything?"

"I didn't feel comfortable going through her personal things before the will was read." Maddy admitted.

"She had a safe deposit box but it only had the deed to the house and her will in it. So we're kind of left hanging." Jack Drake said and snapped his briefcase shut.

"If she thought they were worthless, and I'm sure she checked first, your aunt probably destroyed them." Leland added.

"Surely Aunt Madeline wouldn't have done something like that without checking with either of you." The thought seemed logical. The estate was well arranged in every detail right down to her aunt's funeral. The opposite of what Leland had intimated.

"You keep saying my aunt's estate wasn't very well planned. Except for the missing bonds it seems to be pretty straightforward." Maddy didn't understand.

"Well, that's true to a point. Part of it was and part of it wasn't. It happens more than you think. Like the bonds. We checked the company. C.G. Johnson & Sons went bankrupt some time ago, so I think Leland is right. The bonds probably weren't worth anything, but we'll still keep checking. As for everything else, yes, it's all in order. You have a nice little investment here." Mr. Drake sighed and shrugged.

Maddy couldn't quite figure out if they were making sense or not. Her parents' estate had been small and easily handled by the family attorney. Then she made the mistake of letting Larry Preston handle things for her. She shook her head tiredly at that thought.

"In case you come upon anything you don't understand, or even if you do, please give Leland or me a call. Here's my card. It will help things along greatly, my dear."

Mr. Drake stepped back and put his suit coat on, giving her a sympathetic look. "You have authority now to take possession of your aunt's home and start going through her things. I would give careful consideration to getting rid of that old house, Miss Morris. A big old home like that might become a burden with upkeep and taxes and such. And Leland can probably get you the best deal on unloading it. I'll be in touch, Leland. Good by."

"Thank you, Mr. Drake. I'll keep it in mind." Maddy accepted his handshake and sat down as Leland showed Jack Drake out. She was relieved and a little overwhelmed now that it was over. A strange sadness overcame her as she waited for Leland to return.

"I can hardly believe this is all over and settled, it's rather sad." Maddy said when Leland sat down across from her.

Leland looked at her kindly. "I know, Miss Morris, and I am sorry. Your aunt was a great lady. She must have loved you very much to want you to have all this." He indicated the will and estate papers on the desk.

"She must have. I just hope I can honor her wishes." Maddy said and got up to go.

"Miss Morris, if I may be allowed to ask, what would you do if you did stay in Nielsen? I'm at a loss since we have no library."

"Well, I still think a bed and breakfast would work, but, it's just a thought."

"I see. Well, that's not entirely impossible. It will need some renovations, however. Oh, I nearly forgot, Miss Morris. I found this envelope addressed to you, personally, in your aunt's desk. It's unopened." He added quickly. "We would have had to open it if we hadn't found you, but since we did, here it is." Leland handed the long, white envelope, sealed and addressed in a definitely feminine hand to Maddy.

Fingering the envelope, Maddy put it in her purse. "Thank you, Mr. Lancaster, but I think I'll read it later. It's been an exhausting morning, and I'm drained. I'll let you know if it's important." Maddy stood up quickly. If she didn't get out and get some fresh air she was afraid she would cry for all the things she didn't know about her aunt. After the generous gift she'd been given she knew there was going to be more to handling her aunt's estate than she'd ever anticipated. It was up to her to make this all mean something.

Maybe her sadness was all about the inheritance that she

felt she didn't deservet. It was plain guilt she felt because she hadn't taken the time to know her aunt. The guilt was there to begin with, but her dismissing her aunt way back when she lived here weighed on her mind. She could have been more kind and thoughtful to her. After all, she was her father's favorite aunt.

She wished she had someone to talk to about the way she was feeling. If she handled it right, she wouldn't have to worry about her future and money. But who and where was someone to confide in about her heart? Aunt Polly came to mind, then the thought struck her and she knew where to go, her step quickened and her heart urged her to hurry.

Chapter 5

Maddy pulled her rental car into the neat little corner gas station on Main and Elm Street. She recognized the lone attendant from her morning's blitzkrieg at the truck stop with Alec. This was Tim, one of the guys that had been there. He was quieter than the others, but funny and friendly. She liked him.

Pointing to his embroidered shirt pocket that had Tim on it, she laughed and greeted him. "Hi, Tim, I wasn't sure of the name until I saw your shirt. Alec introduced everyone so fast this morning I wasn't sure I'd remember."

"I know, he told us you were coming to visit. I knew your aunt, too. Nice lady."

They chatted and she asked for directions to the place where she thought she would find the help she was looking for. Tim was happy to oblige.

"Okay, Tim said it wouldn't be hard to find. A mile north

and two miles east, or was that vice versa. Oh, nuts, I wish I wasn't directionally challenged." She was hopeless when it came to directions. "'Find the church,' he said, 'it was close to the church.'" Speaking the words aloud helped and on the next road her tires left pavement and crunched on a gravel drive leading to the gates of the cemetery.

The tall iron gates stood closed but not locked and creaked loudly when Maddy pushed them open. She walked down the gravel drive. The local cemetery and little church her aunt had attended looked as quaint as the rest of the town.

An old oak tree stood on the gently rolling hill that looked down on the town. Here a simple granite stone identified her aunt's final resting place.

Madeline A. O'Keefe
Born April 4, 1919
Died December 23, 2010
A Friend to all

A scroll design and spray of flowers was carved and entwined with her name. Maddy stood silently, tears squeezing out from her tightly closed eyes.

A tenderness and respect she hadn't felt since her parent's deaths enveloped her. These strong feelings were hard to understand about someone she only vaguely knew. A great sadness overcame her and she sat down on a small, cement bench nearby. The day turned warm, a gentle breeze rustled the oak branches overhead and caressed her as if someone were stroking her hair. She lifted her head to the warmth and sighed, taking out the envelope Leland Lancaster had given her. Carefully she opened it and began to read.

My Dear Maddy:

Throughout your life I have followed you growing up. Your parents were good enough to allow me to do that and also live the way I wished, away from the Morris family. I chose not to depend on anyone except myself after my husband died.

Your parents understood my reasons for leaving everything to you, my namesake. There are some things of value. My house and the money left in my accounts should help support you. Go through my personal things and dispose of them as you see fit. The thought of strangers touching my things would distress me greatly..

I have lived a good life and loved my friends and this small town I called home. That is my real wealth. And to you, the daughter I never had, I want you to know I loved you from afar. I remain, lovingly yours,

Madeline Morris O'Keefe

P.S. Do not be angry with your parents for not telling you I was in touch with them. I did not wish to interfere in your busy life.

Maddy's hands shook as she read the paper. She sat up straight and sighed, the letter crumpled in her lap. So many things made sense after reading this. Her parents had told her the many little gifts and books she received on holidays were from her 'secret admirer.'

"Oh, Aunt Madeline, you must have been so lonely at times without your family." Maddy said softly, sadly.

"She never acted lonely. Sometimes just a little sad is

all." Maddy sighed and recognized Alec's voice, but she didn't jump this time.

"Your friend at the gas station tell you were I was?"

Maddy guessed, as he sat down next to her on the small bench and leaned forward, staring at the headstone.

"I shouldn't divulge my sources, but, yes."

Alec's shoulder touched hers and he smiled down at her, "I was going to say I just happened to be driving by."

She leaned back, keenly aware of his presence.

"Sure, you were." Then she smiled sadly and closed her eyes, knowing he was amused by her.

"Old Tim sure appreciated the tip you gave him. He goes to school nights and every penny counts. That was nice of you."

"He earned it. The sign said "No Full Service" and I got full service. He even washed my windows and checked the oil and it's only a rental." Maddy had been impressed.

"Well, consider it Midwestern values. Give the customer a good job and he, or she, will come back. It's a simple rule that works."

"I agree." She said firmly.

They both sat silently, listening to the wind slide through the branches. The people Maddy had been around the last 24 hours were something more than just passing faces. They were starting to mean something to her, she could identify with them. She found herself interested in their lives and hopes and problems as if it mattered to her. Complete strangers and it mattered.

"Everybody needs to feel appreciated, Tim, Bubba, me. We all work hard. But we all like to know there's someone who cares about what we do." Alec said, leaning back, turning his head to gaze at her intently.

"Even you?" She asked, and felt the heat of the look without opening her eyes. He chuckled and his arm slid around the back of the bench.

"Especially me, you know, even men need understanding."

"Even rough, tough, lawmen?" She countered.

"Yes," he answered patiently. "You know, you're quite a girl."

"I was a girl a long time ago." Maddy said softly, feeling the heat of his arm touching hers. Suddenly the bench seemed awfully snug. She pulled herself forward, "I should get going. After a morning like this it just seemed the right place to come."

"Was it rough going with Leland and the Omaha attorney?" Alec's voice was sincere.

"How did you know? I mean I didn't even know the attorney was coming in today?" She was astounded.

"Small towns are like party lines, word gets around fast. I heard it from two people and then Tim." He chuckled at the surprised look on her face.

"Well, did everyone tell you what was in the will, too?" She was a little miffed and stuffed her aunt's letter in her purse. Digging for her keys, she tried to keep her temper under control. She didn't know why she was upset. It was a good guess everyone would assume she was Aunt Madeline's heir. She just wasn't used to people knowing everything personal about her.

"No. Not really, a lot of guessing going on, though."

"I'll bet. Where are my darn keys?" She kept fumbling until he tapped her on the shoulder and handed them to her.

"They were under the bench, you must have dropped them."

Grabbing them in frustration, she shook her head and

sighed, leaning forward. She shouldn't be mad at him or anyone. It was human nature to wonder. He sat quietly with legs outstretched, deep in thought.

She remembered something just then. He'd always been like that, intent. The look on that suntanned face, his blue eyes so expressive as he looked at her. He really hadn't changed a whole lot, she thought to herself, still rugged and stubborn and so darned handsome. It appeared since getting into law enforcement he's become more assertive, at least now she knew how sensitive he was, how he wanted and needed emotional support too.

"A whole lot of things make sense now, especially about my parents and the family stuff. My folks kept in touch with Aunt Madeline and they never said a word. She said she didn't want to depend on anyone or bother anyone. But she could have called on me, I would have come. She must have been so ill and she still didn't call."

"Aunt Polly asked her if there was anyone we could call and she said no, that her lawyer would take care of it. Just bury her where she could look down on the town. So, we did."

"I guess it's my turn to thank you for looking after her. She was lucky to live here, have friends like you. The whole town, it was more than her blood relatives gave her. I feel like I let her down." Suddenly the tears she'd held back let loose. "I feel like I should have done more." She blurted out and sniffled, accepting the white handkerchief he handed her. "Thank you. I hate it when I cry. It doesn't do any good," she said between tears.

Here she had come to have a talk with her great aunt and try and explain how she felt. Instead, she wound up confiding in Alec again. How was this happening? However it was playing out, she was glad he was there.

Alec gently drew her close until his arms encircled her. Holding her so easily, he hadn't realized how he'd ached to have her in his arms. The clock turned back and they were both fifteen again and in the throes of first love. He rested his head on her soft, hair that smelled of strawberries, remembering his fifteen year-old heartache when she left.

By the time Maddy realized what was happening it was too late. She couldn't remember the last time Larry, or anyone had held her so tenderly, so protectively. It made her uneasy to rely on someone she'd just met, but she had to admit it felt good.

She burrowed against his shoulder not wanting him to see her so vulnerable. This was now, not then, not junior high again. Did he just kiss her hair, or had she imagined that? It felt so good to relax, the last tear trickled down her cheek and she leaned into the khaki uniform with an ease that surprised her.

Putting her hands against his broad chest, she shook her head, an apology on her lips.

"I want you to know I don't usually fall apart like this. I don't know what got into me. I'm sorry."

"Don't be. We all have feelings. It's best not to ignore them." Alec murmured right back at her. "We have to handle them the best way we can." His voice was deep with emotion, a sensual hunger in his indigo blue eyes that had Maddy's heart stirring along with his. Bending his head slowly to kiss her, he caught himself and merely rested his stubbly cheek on hers.

Expelling a big sigh, Alec was content to just hold

Maddy and comfort her. Oh, how he wanted to kiss her. He could see she needed time to forgive herself for whatever wrongs she felt she had committed. In his estimation, the guilt of not being here for her aunt was serious for her, but hardly fair. His gentle nudge brought her attention back to the present, back to him.

"Yes, but before you do, Alec, thank you." She smiled through tear-stained lashes.

"I had to do that." He whispered, his eyes smoldering.

"Now come on, before we get in over our heads around here. And right in front of your aunt, too."

"Hey, would you like to get a cold drink or something? It's mighty hot out here." Fanning himself with his hat he took her elbow and guided her through the soft, lumpy grass around the headstones.

She got into her car and he shut the door, resting his arms on the open window close to her face. "How about we get some lunch over at the Trucker's Heaven?"

"I've got a better idea. Why don't we go back to my aunt's? I mean the house, my house, and I'll make us something to eat. I don't feel like being out among people right now."

Eyes bright, he nodded in agreement.

"Sounds good, have you got stuff for sandwiches?"

"Gosh, I forgot, there's not much to fix at my place, haven't been to the grocery store yet. I've got Aunt Polly's coffeecake," she offered. "That's dessert anyway."

"No problem. Tell you what, I'll run through the fast food drive in and meet you there. Burgers and fries?"

"And a malt, I love my malts."

"Chocolate, if I recall. Some things never change." Alec

smiled, leaning his forearms on the open window of her car.

She liked it that he remembered that about her. Gently Maddy put her hand on his forearm, tingling at the feel of his skin. The golden brown hair on his arms was curly and soft and she remembered how soft his hair was along the nape of his neck. The intimate thoughts were coming rapid fire and were intrusive. She had to snap out of it.

"You're being very kind, Deputy McKay."

"It's all in the line of duty, ma'am." The cocky grin surfaced again, "But I got to tell you, Miss Morris, I've never enjoyed my job so much as since you came to town."

This time Maddy didn't blush, instead her heart gave a funny flutter and she found herself wishing he'd kiss her again. He must have read her mind because he gave her a quick peck on the cheek. It was the first time the realization hit her, she was glad she came to this little town.

By the time Alec returned with food from the local drive in, Maddy had the table set with napkins and condiments and changed to jeans and a tee shirt.

"Well, knowing Leland, I'm sure he forgot to even offer you a cup of coffee back at his office. Working with him is no picnic." Swallowing the last drop of his iced tea, Alec sat back and stretched in his chair, watching her.

"Well, he did take me out for breakfast." She pointed a finger at him and laughed, "Remember?"

"Aw, he's not a bad sort, I guess," Alec began, holding his glass out for a refill. "It's just that he's always in the middle of things, always knows just a day ahead when something goes up for sale or someone's in trouble, I don't know. Maybe I'm jaded from working with crooks so much."

Thoughtfully Maddy sat cross-legged in her chair,

filling her glass. "Well, where I come from, the big city, that's called being an astute businessman. Successful. What's wrong with that?"

Alec shrugged and looked around the kitchen before answering. "I don't know. Sometimes I think he's hedging, using his position on the city council and with his job, to profit somehow. But I guess you're right when maybe all he's doing is being a savvy businessman. Like I said, I can't put my finger on it, and I don't tell anyone this either, so keep it to yourself. Just don't let him talk you into anything, okay?"

"Aunt Polly's had dealings with him too. She also warned me about him last night." They grinned at each other. There was a comfortable awareness in being together that Maddy liked. She didn't understand it, but she liked it.

"I still don't know what I'm going to do yet, and there's all this to go through." There wasn't any conviction in her voice. Looking around she suddenly had an overwhelming feeling come over her, the house, all the things in it, were now legally, hers. It was up to her to figure things out, and the problem was getting bigger by the minute.

"So, I guess that means you'll have to stay at least for a little while to dispose of things." Alec said.

Maddy nodded, "Yes and I may need some help with the heavy stuff. You interested?"

"You bet." He chomped on another burger, grinning through pickles and mustard.

"I wound the grandfather clock this morning. I needed some noise in the house besides the local grain and news report. Sounds good, doesn't it?"

"So, you're kind of lonely living in a place like this?"

He picked up the sandwich wrappers and drank the last of his drink.

"No, I'm used to being alone. Well, as alone as having a slightly neurotic best friend can be. I have an apartment in a high rise on Chicago's lakefront. It's nice but small. It's a lot smaller when my best friend Marie crashes with me. She dates a lot and right now she's at odds with her landlord, trying to save for her own place. I wanted to get a dog for company but they aren't allowed in the apartment. But, now I can do what I want. Hang pictures, paint the walls. Maybe get that dog." Walking Alec to the back door she tucked her hands in the back pockets of her jeans and shrugged. "Honestly, listen to me, I'm just dreaming out loud."

"Well, nothing wrong with dreaming. I always wanted a dog too, a hunting dog, but I never had the time or place either, especially being single and working all the time." He turned and paused a moment. "Maddy, I guess I should tell you something. I was married once, briefly, a long time ago. But you seem to know that."

"It's a small town, remember?" She said laughing.

"Well, I hope you don't think I'm butting in, but I'd sure like it if you stayed, at least for a while. I know you'd like the town, Nielsen is a friendly, quiet place but it's full of good people, mostly. Just think about it."

"I will, but no promises. Oh, Alec, look out you'll run into Aunt Polly." Alec had been walking backward talking to Maddy and didn't see Aunt Polly come up behind him.

"Aunt Polly, I'm sorry. I didn't see you." Alec apologized.

"Land sakes, Alec. I'm not surprised since you weren't facing me. Well, you finally got a date. Tell her good by and get going. You're going to be late for work. And don't drive like this, for heaven's sake. They'll be peeling you off the pavement."

"Aunt Polly, just the person I wanted to see." Maddy put an arm around the older woman, and they walked back into the house.

"Good. I'm getting tired over there, sitting and wondering what's going on. From the look on Alec's face, I can guess. But an old gal my age doesn't have time to pussyfoot around, I'm snoopy and I admit it. So there." Aunt Polly said matter-of-factly.

"Well good. I have a huge favor to ask and I hope you're willing." Over iced tea and coffeecake Maddy explained the details of her aunt's will to her new friend and potential neighbor.

"That sure sounds like Madeline, all right. She had a powerful reason to do the things she did. I don't understand this thing with her family, even tried to talk her into making up but she said most everyone was dead. Funny thing, she never seemed bitter or spiteful, just plain wouldn't talk about it."

"Maybe we'll learn more when we go through her things. That's the favor. Would you help me, please?" Desperately Maddy clasped Aunt Polly's hand. "Now that it's official, I feel less like an intruder. I know she would like you to have something special to remember her by, too, but I just need your help so much."

Aunt Polly sat silent for a moment looking around.

"I sat in this kitchen many times over the years, shared a lot with Madeline. She was with me when my only child, Frank, died in a farm accident in 1969. That was the last of my family, too. Made us kindred spirits you might say. Madeline was a fine lady and a good friend. I don't need anything else to remember her by."

"I wish I could have known her like that." Maddy said softly, "You're lucky."

Aunt Polly sighed and wiped her glasses. "No. The town and I were the lucky ones to have known her."

Putting the fragile spectacles back on, she slapped her knee and leaned forward. "Yes, she always was the first one to help. Now maybe I can repay her kindness. So, I'll help you. As for a remembrance, well, I got a heart full of memories. That's enough for me, that, and now you." Sipping her tea, she shook her head and chuckled. "I'm talking your ear off aren't I? So windy I could dry a load of laundry in front of me. Just one more thing, you're a good person. Your aunt knew that or she wouldn't have kept track of you. She liked Alec, thought he was a fine judge of character." Her voice was full of pride when she mentioned the cocky young deputy.

Maddy didn't say much but recognized what might be an effort at matchmaking in progress. If anything, her new friend appeared honest and straightforward. It was apparent she addored Alec, too.

"Yep, he's so much like my own boy, I often overlook his shortcomings. He's got them you know. But he's a good man. Can't understand why that gal would leave him, how anyone could hurt him. Oh well, water under the bridge."

Absently, Aunt Polly nodded and sat back in the rocking chair, hands clasped over her stomach.

While cleaning up the dishes, Maddy thought about what Aunt Polly meant when she talked of someone hurting Alec. It had to be about his divorce. Debating whether to mention it or not, she decided to wait a while. They all had things in their past they didn't like to talk about.

Chapter 6

In Chicago Maddy jogged with at least one friend or a group of her apartment neighbors would invite her to join them. There was always a safety issue and running in numbers was best living in the big city.

It paid to be careful. She was in rush hour crowds at lunch and an unseen hand jerked her shoulder bag off and disappeared. That time she was angry rather than scared because she couldn't do anything. It was all very frustrating and expensive. Her I.D. had been in it and she had to have all her locks and phone number changed. It was a big, time-consuming hassle.

The day after she officially became owner of her aunt's property, she rose early and decided to jog around Nielsen. Since she didn't know anyone who jogged, she looked around tentatively and stepped out on the porch stretching to prepare to run. Luckily she had remembered her gym bag with black running shorts, a light tee shirt and her favorite running shoes in it.

Maddy started out easily down the street past Aunt Polly's, waving when she saw her peek out the door. She headed towards the town square and luxuriated at the freedom from worry about traffic or being mugged. The stores were just coming alive for the day. She recognized many of the merchants and waved as she jogged past them, heading for a country road that led out of town.

Maddy found herself becoming addicted to everything about the country life. She almost hated to turn back for the day, but she did. Just by coincidence she passed the small sheriff's office and quickly backpedaled to stand, jogging in place, in front of the plate glass window.

It didn't take long for Alec to notice and come out.

"Hey, you're up and out early this morning." He looked enviously at her. "Wish I could join you."

"Join me? Hey, I just went two miles out and two miles back. I'm on my way home. How about you? You look a tad out of shape there deputy." She teased and poked a finger at his stomach.

"Hey, I'm a busy man."

"Well, crime rate so high you can't jog sometime?" She panted, bending at the waist to catch her breath.

He scratched his jaw and smiled, "I'm off duty tomorrow. You want to put your money where your mouth is?"

She shrugged and started out past him. "I'll be by here at seven sharp, then breakfast at my place, if you can keep up."

"I can keep up. That's a challenge if I ever heard one. I'll be here, waiting." He called out after her then looked at his reflection in the window and rubbed his stomach. "I'm not out of shape, either!"

It was the first of many mornings they shared jogging and then home to bran muffins and orange juice in Maddy's sunny kitchen. The routine became comfortable and she liked how it made her feel, like a part of something. When Alec couldn't make it, she really missed those ragged police academy sweat clothes and that insufferable grin as he tried to run her into the ground. But on his busy days she used the time to go through her aunt's things with Aunt Polly.

"I sure understand all the wonderful books I got over the years now. Aunt Madeline was quite the connoisseur when it came to reading." Her hand passed over the richly bound books lining the walls.

"It's probably why you became a librarian, too." Aunt Polly winked at her as she dusted the volumes. "You know she used to have a whole set of expensively bound books, right here by the door. I don't see them anywhere now."

"Are you sure, about the books? They might be in the attic. Maybe she put them away or sold them."

"No. No, them was the first books she bought years ago, classics, she called them. Real expensive and she treated them like they was made out of gold. Your aunt said she'd never get rid of them." Aunt Polly's suspicions made Maddy feel uneasy. "Are you thinking what I'm thinking?"

Aunt Polly nodded with a knowing look.

"That's what I'm getting at. Only Leland and I have been in here that I know of. Makes a body wonder what else is missing. Have you found her jewelry box yet?"

"Well, just this one." Maddy pulled an oriental, red-lacquered box from the roll-top desk. "I wonder what it's doing in her desk instead of her bedroom."

"That's not her jewelry box, at least not the one she showed me." A frown creased Aunt Polly's face. She looked up and down the tall bookcases on either side of the doors in the library, dusting as she went.

"Well, I don't know where this one came from but Madeline's was bigger and made of black leather. There were gold corners and a lock on it."

Gingerly Maddy snapped open the lock and lifted the lid. Only a tangle of pearls and some cheap costume jewelry lay in the bottom. The top part had a cameo set of a pin and earrings in it.

"I don't know where this cheap stuff came from, but this was her favorite." Aunt Polly said softly and picked up the cameo. "She told me her husband gave them to her, wore them all the time. There's a picture album around somewhere of him and her, and she's wearing them in the picture. She had a lot of nice jewelry, expensive, too."

"This is the only jewelry I've seen around." Maddy said uneasily. "What about her husband, did she ever talk about him?"

Aunt Polly handed her back the cameo with a sigh. She dusted slowly, her eyes soft as she remembered.

"She said she met him in Omaha back in the late 30s or so. They got married, never had any kids. He was drafted in World War Two and never made it back. It just about broke her heart and she moved here for a fresh start. She told me he didn't have any family and she didn't claim any." Aunt Polly shrugged, lost in her thoughts, "His name was Franklin, Franklin O'Keefe. That's all I know."

Maddy jumped out of her chair and went into the parlor where she recalled seeing a plush, velvet photo album in an old Victrola cabinet. Laying it open on the desk, she and Aunt Polly gazed at the old photographs.

"Here, here's the picture of Franklin and your Aunt Madeline. Nice looking couple, they were. She used to have this sitting on her dresser."

A handsome man sat with her Aunt Madeline. He was in an Army uniform and she wore a simple white gown with high neckline and lace veil framing her face. The cameo broach was centered at her throat and she had on the matching pierced earrings. Her own striking resemblance to her young aunt astounded Maddy. They looked alike, right down to the way she wore her short hair.

"Yep, you two could have been sisters." Aunt Polly nodded.

"That's incredible; we do look alike, don't we?"

Maddy smiled and touched the photo. "You said he died in the war. Then where is he buried?" Maddy closed the book carefully and looked at her friend.

"Yes, that war killed a lot of good men. I think Madeline said he died at Omaha Beach, she always thought it was ironic that a man from Omaha, Nebraska, should die in a battle with the same name. I think he was buried overseas."

They cleaned the rest of the afternoon in thoughtful silence, wondering about the lives Franklin and Madeline had in such a star-crossed time, ending so sadly.

They were stretched out on the wicker lawn furniture when Alec drove up after work, too exhausted to move. They simply waved for him to join them, pointing to a frosty pitcher of lemonade sitting between them. Maddy was on the lounger, her hair covered in a red bandana and Aunt Polly relaxed in a curved rocker.

"What do we have here? Two ladies too pooped to pop?" Alec teased, sitting down at the foot of Maddy's lounger.

"For your information, young man, we've got the entire downstairs cleaned and sorted." Aunt Polly informed him and then yawned.

"My aunt was neat enough," Maddy continued, "but she saved everything." She poured a glass of lemonade for Alec and refilled hers.

"I'm glad you stopped by, Alec," Aunt Polly sat up straight and seemed to forget her fatigue. "Well, are you going to tell him, or am I?" She glanced at Maddy.

"Tell me what?" Alec looked from one to the other in anticipation. He placed an arm over Maddy's slim leg in a familiar gesture. His warm skin on her leg sent prickles up her spine. She liked it when he acted comfortable around her.

"Oh, Aunt Polly seems to think some of my aunt's things are missing." Maddy said uneasily.

"Well, are they missing, or not?" Alec took on a professional manner as he sipped on his drink and stared at them intently. "Tell me about it."

"Well, we came across a small, red jewelry box and Aunt Polly said my aunt had a big, black jewelry box with valuable pieces like a strand of pearls, ruby ring, diamond and gold broach. I don't know, I never saw them of course, but so far all we've found was some cheap costume jewelry, oh, and the cameo pin and earrings." Maddy shrugged, feeling uncomfortable.

"Are you sure, Aunt Polly?" Alec asked, his tone serious.

"Of course I'm sure. Oh, and don't forget the leather bound books, they're gone, too. She told me she'd never get rid of them. I wouldn't make that up."

He overlooked her sarcasm with a shake of his head when Aunt Polly sat back with arms crossed, rocking vigorously. Maddy and Alec exchanged glances and he patted Aunt Polly's knee consolingly.

She shook a finger and scolded him. "Don't you patronize me, young man, I may be old and I might be a little deaf but one thing's certain, I know my friend's jewelry. Except for the cameo set, it's not here."

"Well, we still have all the upstairs to go through, yet." Maddy interjected, trying to smooth the situation over.

"I agree. But this happens when houses sit empty. If they don't show up we better start an investigation. I'll check a few places tomorrow." Alec said.

"I'm sure they'll show up, I'll ask Leland about it too."

"I know what he'll say. 'My secretary looks after that.'" Aunt Polly mimicked and stopped rocking. "I'm sorry, but I just don't trust that man. He wanted me to turn over everything I own for him to manage not long ago, I told him I been handling my affairs all my life and can handle them now. He left mad. I don't think Madeline would have let him either if he hadn't got a hold of her when she was so sick. Right after he started taking care of her he bought that big old car he drives. Might be a coincidence, might not be."

"Oh, Aunt Polly, he has to be honest in his business or no one would go to him. We have to give him the benefit of the doubt." Maddy shook her head.

"What about the break-in?" Alec said suddenly, snapping his fingers.

"Someone had been inside, but nothing was disturbed so we blamed kids just playing a prank. I remember because I was out chasing rustlers at the Thedford farm. Whoever broke in might have taken the jewelry."

"Rustlers?" Maddy interrupted disbelief on her face.

Alec nodded. "No jokes please, we have high-tech rustlers now, complete with computers and 18-wheel rigs for the getaway."

"I always pictured them as bad guys in black hats riding horses and swooping down on the cattle herds. Trucks and computers are not very romantic."

"Cattle rustling is big business, it's hardly romantic. They've even taken a couple shots at me." Alec replied dryly.

Maddy's shocked look made him laugh.

"Don't worry, they missed. But, getting back to the break in, I don't know if it's such a good idea for you to stay here alone, Maddy. Honestly, you don't even have a cell phone yet. Maybe someone knew about the missing bonds and came across the jewelry. They may decide to come back for more." He shook his head and looked at her seriously, no good-natured teasing in his eyes.

Maddy shook her head immediately. "I am not going to let someone chase me out of my home. Plus, we don't even know if that's what happened. You said yourself you thought it was just kids. No, absolutely not. I made a promise to myself that I was going to run my own life from now on. I intend to."

Maddy refused to listen. "No, it's settled. I'll take every precaution but I am not leaving my home. I can go get a new phone and I'll lock my doors. I don't want to take a chance on Aunt Polly getting drug into this."

Alec looked from one to the other, "Then let me stay here with you." At her dubious laugh, he waved his hands and nodded. "Okay, okay, I know how that sounds, and the last time I made the offer I was kidding, sort of. But, I'll sleep on the couch and be gone before you get up."

Aunt Polly chuckled, "I don't even buy that one, but it was a good try, Alec."

"Aunt Polly, please, I'm trying to be serious here. Neither of you seem to realize that these thieves could be dangerous. I just don't want you to be alone."

"Are you both through?" Maddy said with hands on hips, "You are blowing this all out of proportion. We'll go on like we planned, finish cleaning things out. You'll check some things out you said, Alec. Then and only then will I make any big decisions. If I'm going to run the minute there might be trouble here in Nielsen, I should have just stayed in Chicago. I know there's trouble there."

"Man, you are a stubborn woman." Alec growled, his eyes dark and disapproving.

"Sorry, but I'm not leaving." She folded her arms, ending the discussion.

"Well, would you consider leaving the house for the evening?" He said with just a tinge of sarcasm before he smiled at her.

"I don't know, what do you mean by that?" She asked suspiciously. "I said I'm not leaving, Alec and I meant it so don't try and trick me."

"I'm not going to trick you. I came over here to begin with to see if you're up to dinner tonight? I can dig out my old yearbook later, maybe a little reminiscing?"

"Oh, I don't know. I'm a mess. We've been working all afternoon." Maddy's first impulse was to pass, but something made her consider going. If she wasn't going to run scared from burglars, she sure wasn't going to be intimidated by Alec McKay. She just had to prove she could take care of her house and her heart. Maddy watched Alec's expressive eyes as he anticipated a refusal.

"Come on. We'll take Aunt Polly for a chaperone. I'm beginning to think you just don't want to go out with me."

"You've been out with Leland. You can go out with me. Come on, you're going to give me a complex." Alex pouted.

Maddy was beginning to think something was wrong with her. A great looking guy asks her out and she won't go? It was more than that. It was year's worth of uncertainty and betrayal from guys that always hurt her. Was it just too soon, or was she so scared she would take that chance?

Maddy considered it, running her finger along the edge of the lounger. "Okay, but this better not be some kind of trick to keep me from coming back here."

Leaning over her still-stretched out form, he took in every inch of the long, slim legs in short cut-off jeans.

His closeness was overpowering and Maddy swallowed hard. He'd surely move back so she could get up. But he didn't. Their eyes locked, their faces so close she could feel his warm breath on her face.

"If you want me to go, let me get up."

"Who said I wanted to let you go?" Alec leaned down as his lips touched her cheek. She could feel the corners of his mouth go up, his lips seeking hers softly. Maddy dissolved into his kiss with hesitant but pliant lips. The kiss felt secure and warm as he gathered her up in his arms. It felt so right, so familiar, too good to stop.

The faint honking of a horn finally separated them. A pick-up with familiar faces pulled up in front of the house. The hollering and hooting ended the moment, and reluctantly Alec turned towards them "Boy, you guys have lousy timing. What do you want?"

"Hey, Miss Maddy, how are you? Hey, Lawman, we just saw your car and thought we'd drop in and say "hi". Good thing, I think we saved her from a fate worse than death." The laughter began again and Alec planted a quick kiss on her flushed face.

"I'll pick you up at seven," he said, and she ducked behind the screen door waving at his friends.

"Don't forget I like chocolate ice cream." She retorted and shut the door firmly behind her.

Walking out to the street, he leaned on the fence and talked to his friends for a few minutes before they all drove off.

Chapter 7

At 7 p.m. sharp, Alec McKay stepped out of a shiny, red pick up. A crisp red and black plaid cowboy shirt covered his wide shoulders and snug blue jeans seemed molded to his body. Shiny black cowboy boots and black felt cowboy hat finished off the outfit.

"Hi, there." He met her with a low throaty greeting as she opened the door.

"Hi, yourself. I'm kind of worried. I thought the good guys wore white hats not black." She teased and stepped back to let him in.

His sexy smile returned and he chuckled at her joke. "You clean up good, yourself. Different look without the head scarf. But good." He assured her.

It took her a moment to look at him and not see the deputy's uniform and gun, but only a moment. His clothes didn't just look like a sharp outfit on Alec, it was Alec. He looked the way he had in her young girl dreams and now she was seeing it for real.

"Believe it or not, I hear that a lot. But deputies are people too, and I like black for evening wear. Looks like you do, too. I like what you're wearing very much, Maddy."

She gave a little curtsy, holding out the full gathered cotton skirt, black with tiny little flowers and a white peasant blouse that slipped casually off her shoulders. A bright yellow silk flower sat tucked behind her ear, accenting the color of her hair.

"Thank you. Well, I guess we better go out, we're so well-coordinated."

He quickly turned and recovered a paper sack from the plant stand by the door. "Your wish is my command, my dear lady. Chocolate ice cream."

"Good. I'm quite serious about ice cream. I'll stick it in the freezer and then we can go."

As they walked out the door into the fresh night air, he made sure the door was locked and then whispered in her ear, "I'm getting quite serious, too, about you. It's why I don't like you staying here alone."

"I thought we were through with that discussion. Just don't get too sure of yourself, deputy. I've been mugged before. I can take care of myself."

"It's just plain Alec when I'm off duty, Maddy, and I wish you'd reconsider. I'm positive you can take care of yourself but you don't have to prove it. If anyone did break in you could argue them to death." He sighed and raised his eyebrows. "Okay, I won't push it. Let's just have a good time."

They had a wonderful meal at a little steak house in Grand Island. The drive was relaxing and Alec's company was enjoyable to say the least. He was still the flattering, teasing, young boyfriend of years ago, but with a mature side to him that fascinated her.

They lingered over wine and the talk came easily, and later a small band started to play. Maddy reluctantly let him take her in his arms for a dance.

"Remember the last time we danced?" Alec's blue eyes were sexy in the soft light, filled with memories.

"Vaguely."

"Oh, come on, you do, too." He swung her around smoothly.

"Okay, yes, the Homecoming Dance. So?"

"So? You can be so stubborn. If you hadn't moved away we might be married right now instead of just getting to know each other again."

"Well, so can you. I could say the same if you had just written or called me. Never mind, let's not go there. Not to change the subject, but does dancing come in handy for police work?"

"After tonight I'm going to see to it that it's a requirement. You realize if you hadn't gone out with me tonight I was going to have to arrest you for speeding or something." Without missing a beat he rested his chin on her soft hair and breathed the light scent of her perfume.

Leaning back, Maddy stared at him suspiciously, "I just bet you'd try that. For your information, I don't speed."

"Well, you know that," he twirled her around once and brought her up close to his face, "and I know that, but if it's what it would have taken I might have tried it. Besides, why are you shying away from me? It's not like we never met, or you can't trust me. Is that it? You're scared of me," he challenged.

He twirled her once again and wrapped her in his arms as she swung back. Maddy couldn't tell what the look on his face meant. If she didn't watch it she was going to ruin the whole evening, maybe the whole relationship that might be coming.

"I am not scared of you or anyone. For goodness sakes, I don't want to dance anymore if you're going to say things like that. But you know what? I don't know. Silly as it sounds, I feel so overwhelmed sometimes that I don't know how I feel."

"And you say I'm stubborn. For your information I thought about you a lot after you left, really, I did. But, it's different for guys. Guys don't just sit down and pour our hearts out in a letter." He shrugged and grinned and pulled her back into their dance.

"Yeah, right, you thought about me for oh, five minutes probably. Then you moved on to Linda Wiese."

"Linda Wiese? How'd you know that?" He laughed and gave her a little hug. She pushed him back to arm's length stiffly.

"A teenage girl who moves always leaves spies behind."

"Nadine Pfeifer wrote you, didn't she?" His tone was accusing but amused. "And I took her to senior prom."

"Well, at least she and Linda did write me. This is more than I can say for the guy I told I loved at the Homecoming dance."

"Hey, I meant to write more, and I called. I did write once or twice, I think, and, okay, I called twice. Not good enough, huh? Hey, cut me some slack, Girl, will you?" He would not give up. His eyes were taut with the teasing she was handing back. "I'll make it up to you tonight." He bent to kiss her but she had already backed out of his arms.

"I think we ought to get going. I'm expecting my friends to call from Chicago tonight."

"Hey, dance with me just until the song ends, please?

It's the only excuse I have to hold you without you getting mad at me. You're not mad now are you?" His words were beguiling.

"Look. I admit there are some old feelings here tonight, with us, like this, but, but, let's not get in a hurry."

"In a hurry? We've got to make up for lost time." Alec said, his grip on her waist tightening. "Tell me."

"Honestly, should I call you deputy or Alec? I wouldn't have a chance if you were interrogating me for real. We've just gotten reacquainted and you're trying to make me confess. I don't know how long I'm going to be here so I don't want to rush into anything. Let's not get hurt, again."

"Lady," he traced her kissable lips with a finger and looked deeply into the emerald green eyes, "I don't know what it is about you, maybe it's the past we share, but I think I'm going to get hurt no matter what."

His statement caught Maddy off-guard and when he pulled her close she just leaned into him and slowly slid her arms around his neck. The short hair at the nape of his neck was as soft as she recalled and she stroked it ever so slowly as he held her swaying in time to the romantic music.

The second song started and they didn't stop. With a sensual move, his hands encircled her waist and he pulled her lithe body close to his. They danced like that for a long time after the music stopped and the dance floor had cleared. Feeling others watching them, Alec stepped back and grinned sheepishly at her. Her cheeks were flushed as he escorted her off the dance floor.

"I see what you mean, deputy." Maddy used the term affectionately and he didn't correct her this time.

The ride back to Nielsen was quiet and serious. The full moon gave everything a surrealistic aura. Alec drove leisurely, passing darkened farms and obscure blobs of livestock in shadowy fields. Only a few cars passed them in the late hour. Occasionally they would look up, their eyes locked in unspoken emotions. He covered her hand with his on the seat and pulled her close.

"So, if you decide to stay, what do you think you'll do, just for the sake of conversation?" He quickly added.

The question had obviously been bothering him and now was flung out in the open. His gaze stayed glued to the road.

Leaning her head back, she let the night air blow languidly across her face, feeling seductive and intoxicating all at the same time. She didn't know what she wanted. Looking over at his serious profile she wanted to impulsively throw herself over to him and kiss him just to get him to stop asking her that, but she didn't. His hand tightened over hers.

"I honestly don't know, Alec. There's so much to consider. When I came out here I didn't think you'd still be around, that you, we, us would even be an option. This call is from Marie. She's been looking after my apartment and said the garage called and my car is done. And, well, I was expecting a big promotion, hopefully she'll know something. If I get it I may go back."

"Is that all, your apartment, your car, your promotion? It's all stuff."

"Well, it's all important to me." She fired back defensively. It had been important to her only a week ago, now she wasn't so sure. Alec's casual attitude about it didn't help much. "This is a big decision, Alec, to pull up roots and just move away from everything you've ever known. Plus head of a department would be good for my career."

"All I know is you got a lot going for you right here, Maddy." His finger tapped the steering wheel impatiently and Maddy raised her eyebrows quickly from the landscape to Alec. "In the short time you've been here you've made friends, knocked me off my feet, acquired a home, and, well, kind of established yourself. You got to admit it's safer than that crazy city life you have."

"Hey, that crazy city life was my whole life up until now. My friends are there, too, Buffy, Skippy, Marie and, and even Larry, too, I guess. They're like family." Even though Maddy was unsure, she couldn't help feeling defensive.

"What about this Larry back in Chicago? Do I need to worry about him?" For an instant his mood sharpened.

"For your information, they are very, very good friends from college. Well, except for Larry. He came later. Skippy and Buffy and Marie and I grew up together, and stayed together. They're not any odder than your being friends with Terry, Bubba and Tim. And as for Larry, it's none of your business. And how dare you insult my friends without even knowing them." Her face felt as red as her hair.

"Okay, I see I stepped on your toes with that one. I meant to be funny. I'm sorry. But you have to admit it sounds a bit strange, I mean is this Skippy a guy or a girl? There's a peanut butter named Skippy."

"Alec McKay. It's a guy, a man. Skippy is just an old family nickname. His real name is Trevor Benson the Fourth and his parents gave him that name when he was a baby. Just who named Bubba, Bubba? The football team?" At his sudden startled look Maddy had to laugh, "There. I rest my case."

"Okay, okay, truce. Just like we can't pick our relatives, we can't change our friends' names to suit us. But really, Skippy?" Shaking his head in his effort to get the last word in, Alec chuckled and Maddy folded her arms stubbornly stifling a laugh. It was irritating how he made her laugh when she really didn't want to.

When he suggested they stop at a local bar called the "Watering Hole" she hesitated. It looked crowded, probably with all his friends.

"Come on. Let's see if you're as accepting of my friends as you say I should be with yours. They're all nice, really, you might even know some of them."

The place was in full swing. Maddy let Alec lead the way through the rollicking crowd. The smell of barbecue drifted lazily and the music was country and western, which she liked, all to the tune of clinking glasses and laughter. Everyone greeted her and her popular escort warmly. Begrudgingly she had to admit she felt more at ease than she'd thought she would.

Suddenly a loud bellow directed them to a corner table where the same bunch of guys sat that had stopped in front of her house this afternoon. Thirsty, Maddy took a big drink of the beer that someone had handed her, these were the guys who had seen Alec kiss her, only now they were accompanied by their wives and girlfriends. She took another drink. She was going to need it.

A pretty Blonde stood beside the table talking to Bubba, her face lit up when she saw Alec, but in the next instant she saw Maddy and her expression changed. Alec saw her about the same time and grinned, taking Maddy's hand and leading her through the boisterous crowd.

"Ah, Becky Snider's here, you, remember Becky, from school?"

"Becky, Becky Snider? No, I don't think so." Maddy was jostled into Alec by the unruly crowd.

"Yeah, well, it's Becky Roberts now. She's divorced. We've dated a little." Maddy stiffened and looked over at Becky who was laughing and visiting with the group while casting an eye in their direction.

"What exactly does 'kinda' dating someone, mean?" She asked, trying to stop and talk in the bustling crowd. Finally she stopped short. "Alec, I know how this works when you're 'kinda' dating, how could you do this? Get me out of here now, please."

"Maddy, listen, Becky and I are not going together, honest. If she was waiting for me tonight, it was her idea, not mine. The guys probably didn't tell her I had a date tonight, which I do sometimes. We all just meet up here some nights for a drink. Who's here is who's here. No formal invitations or dates. I swear. Besides, she was supposed to work tonight."

"Well, that certainly makes it okay. She must feel awful, and I feel like a definite third wheel." They were pushed together by the crowd and finally made their way over to the table.

"It's not like that, I tell you. Aw, come on. I want you to meet my friends." He whispered in her ear. "Even more, I wanted my friends to see what a classy woman, I fell for. Lady, if you can't tell, I really like you by now. I care, Maddy." He looked from his friends to her, his big, blue eyes as sure as each morning's sunrise. Once again, Maddy gave in.

"Thanks, Maddy. You won't be sorry."

"I hope not. Who do you think Becky will hit first, you or me?" Maddy said loud enough for him to hear. Alec just shook his head, finally finding a couple of open seats at the table.

"Hi, everyone, some of you already know Maddy, Madeline Morris, except for the girls. Well, maybe you did go to school with her. Anyway, everyone, this is Maddy."

"And you remember Becky Snider, Becky Roberts now?"

Alec nodded toward the Blonde watching them both intensely. Becky nodded and smiled, but said nothing. Maddy thought she looked a bit familiar.

The music started and some of the couples got up to dance. Becky chatted with Tim at the end of the table, still giving an occasional glance their way. Maddy couldn't tell if she was upset or not, just cool. Finally, she nudged Alec's leg under the table until he looked at her.

"You could ask Becky to dance, she looks as if she'd like to. It would be a nice gesture." Maddy whispered in Alec's ear.

"Are you going to be in Nielsen long, Maddy?" One of the girls asked the tired question innocently. Maddy wanted to answer honestly and took a deep breath and smiled.

"I really don't know yet. My great aunt left me her house, it's the big, two-story on Main." Slowly, easily they all began to get acquainted and Alec was right, they were really nice and she liked them, even Bubba.

When the song ended Alec came back to the table and Becky began to dance with Tim. Alec squeezed in beside Maddy and reached for her hand under the table.

"That's was a nice thing to suggest, dancing with Becky, I mean."

"Underneath all that stubbornness and muscles is a nice man, too. I recognize that." Maddy answered, keeping her eyes on the dancers. "Maybe we should dance now."

"I'd like that even more."

He walked her out to the dance floor and she moved into his arms as if they were two pieces that fit together perfectly.

"Yes, Becky's nice. We'd only dated a couple times. She's still carrying a torch for her ex, anyway."

"I knew you'd have fun." He said and twirled her once more around the floor. A few minutes later, she excused herself to go to the ladies room.

"Oh man, that could be a recipe for disaster. But you already danced with Becky, was she okay about Maddy?" Bubba rolled his eyes in anticipation of what could happen in there.

Several girls were leaving as Maddy entered. Becky came in as Maddy applied fresh lipstick and brushed through her hair. Turning, Maddy leaned against the vanity, arms crossed casually, returning the stare.

"I'm sorry if my being here makes things uncomfortable for you." Maddy's tone was firm but sincere.

"Why should I be uncomfortable?" She finally looked away.

"Alec told me when we came in you two had been dating." Their eyes met in the mirror.

"So? We dated. It's a fact. But nothing serious came of it, at least not for him." She blotted her lipstick and shrugged, looking at Maddy in the mirror. "He's still looking. At least he was."

"Even so, I found myself in the same position a while back, and I know how it feels. I just wanted you to know I may not be here much longer."

"It doesn't matter if you're here or not. My ex-husband and I are going to try again for the kids' sake if nothing else. So please don't worry."

"Well, then, okay."

"It was nice of you to say that. Boy, it's kind of hard not to like you." Becky smiled and brushed her long, golden hair. "Really, don't worry about it, we had some fun but that's all."

"You're not just saying that?"

"No. Not that I wouldn't have wanted it to be more, but it just wasn't there for us, not like when he looks at you. That hasn't changed since high school, I can tell that already. It's like turning back the clock with you and him at the Homecoming Dance. Remember?" Becky chuckled and Maddy slowly smiled.

Maddy blushed as Becky tucked the brush in her purse and nodded knowingly at her.

"About his divorce..." Maddy hesitated to ask but couldn't help herself.

"He'll tell you when he's ready."

"Yes, I guess he will." Maddy said as she and Becky parted company. Suddenly the details of his divorce just didn't seem very important anymore.

Alec was watching for her. His eyes automatically went from one to the other. Becky just smiled and gave him a nod and disappeared in the crowd. Maddy looked at him calmly.

"So, I told you Becky was cool with things. Not to be nosy, but you were in there an awful long time."

"Oh, I was? I didn't notice." Maddy started back to the table with Alec following close behind.

"How did Becky act? I mean, she acted like everything was cool. Is that what she told you?"

"Yes, she did." Maddy acted distracted.

"So, what did you talk about?"

"Oh, just girl talk, marriages, divorces, relationships."

"You talked about all that, just now?" Alec shook his head in disbelief and frowned.

"Oh, that and more. Why?"

"Well, you know. I mean, you thought Becky was upset. I was pretty sure she wasn't. But, guys miss the point sometimes. You told me that and apparently I have missed it tonight."

"She's really a very nice person. And I do remember her from junior high now, and we had some of the same memories after all."

"Were they good ones, I hope." He held out her chair for her as she sat down.

Maddy thought for a moment, a slow smile spreading on her lips. Nodding, she looked at him with a new sense of clarity, "Yes, they were," she said, and she meant it.

Chapter 8

The phone was madly ringing when Maddy and Alec came in. Alec went to the kitchen and got the ice cream out while Maddy went to the phone in the hallway. Sitting on the stiff, wooden chair telephone stand she watched as Alec made his way around the kitchen getting spoons and bowls for their ice cream as she answered the call.

"Yes. Hello, Marie. How are you? How's everything at the apartment? Yes, what's not to be fine with two philodendrons and an answering machine?"

"Skippy and Buffy are really going to do it, they're really getting married! Isn't that wonderful! When? Where? Oh, you'll have to tell me all the details later."

"I really don't know, Marie, there's a lot to do yet. Besides, I still have vacation time left and I'm going to take it all since I didn't get the promotion." Maddy hated to hedge with her dear friend, but she could only look at Alec standing in the doorway and realize there was no comparison. He was right; it was just stuff in her life. She held the phone away from her ear, Alec could hear every word.

"Can't you just put the place up for sale and leave it in the hands of the realtor? You don't have to be there, do you, Maddy? You at least have it up for sale don't you?" Marie's voice was getting shrill.

"Well, no, not yet. I still have to go through my aunt's things. There's this darling little neighbor lady who insists everyone call her Aunt Polly, who's helping me."

"Aunt Polly? What did you do, fall into a Tom Sawyer time warp or something, Maddy?" The ridicule at Aunt Polly's expense wasn't funny and Maddy felt uncomfortable and terribly torn between her new friend and her old one. She continued the conversation half-heartedly.

"I guess things sound a little strange unless you're here. But she's very nice." She stood, unused to being tethered to a landline when she wanted to pace her frustration off. Marie could be frustrating sometimes.

Suddenly it dawned on Maddy that Marie was selfish. All their friendship, Marie had been the one who chose the movie, the restaurant, the party they would go to. Maddy knew it and didn't mind, then. It was just her friend's personality.

"Are there any good looking farm boys around there, Maddy?

I'll bet you're bored to tears out in the sticks." Marie hadn't even realized Maddy wasn't listening.

"Larry's been asking about you? Did you hear me?"

"Yes, I heard, Marie, and I don't know why you'd think I care about where he is." Her snappish tone shocked Marie.

"Well, as a matter of fact, he said you haven't returned the ring and he thinks you're still engaged."

"The ring is on my entry table right where I left it with a note. I told him the engagement is off. We are not engaged and that's final. Okay? So don't bring up his name to me anymore. And, please make sure he gets the note if he asks again."

As excited as she'd been to hear from her friend back home, Maddy suddenly was becoming very tired with this telephone call.

"Well, I think you're protesting too much. He looks great and he misses you." Larry was on Marie's mind but Maddy's thoughts centered on the handsome face of one complicated, but sexy deputy who had entered her life so casually and wanted her to stay in Nielsen. Larry Preston seemed like a million years ago.

"Well, I hope you didn't tell him where I was. I don't want to talk to him, much less argue with him."

"Well, it did, kind of, slip out the other night at the concert in the park, Maddy. Sorry."

"He doesn't know my number here and don't you give it to him. I don't have anything to talk to him about." Maddy could have wrapped the phone cord around her insensitive friend's neck. "Marie, you know what he put me through before I left, I just don't need any more people telling me what I should do with my life right now."

"Hey, Maddy, I'm sorry, really. You never said not to say anything to anyone. You all right, you sound weird."

"I'm fine, Marie. Just a little tired. I went out tonight, and I had such a good time." She looked at Alec sitting in the kitchen patiently. "I'll probably see the realtor tomorrow or something, I'll call later this week."

"You better. The sooner you get back to civilization the better, girl. Your boss called and you didn't get the promotion. But that shouldn't change anything. Just come home. We all miss you. Talk to you later. Bye."

"Ice cream's melting." Alec handed her the bowl. His was empty. Sitting down she took a bite and rested her head on one hand.

"I suppose you heard."

"It's kind of hard not to. Sorry about losing the promotion. Your friend's pushing for you to go back to Chicago and take up life as you know it, huh? Was that Buffy or Skippy?" He gave a wry grin.

"You heard me call her Marie, silly. I'm sure law enforcement calls for eavesdropping occasionally too, huh?" The ice cream was totally melted and she put it down. "I didn't think I'd get the promotion anyway. I don't know how to play politics well enough. Or, maybe I really didn't want it."

"I didn't realize that you were getting pushed and pulled so much from all of us. I know I want you to stay, but that's selfish. You have to make up your own mind, Maddy, not for me or them. I had to learn that too. I got married right out of high school for all the wrong reasons, trying to please everyone but myself. I just didn't realize she didn't love me enough to try and work it out. It turned out to be a mess until I took control of my own life." He spoke softly, very wisely and gave her a wink. "I'll try and not push, too. But you let me know if this Larry gives you trouble."

"I can handle Larry. Do you have to go already?" He got up and put his black cowboy hat on. His smile was beguiling and he planted a warm kiss on her cheek, cupping her chin in his hand.

"Yes, I have to work early tomorrow, too. Besides, you need some time to yourself to think. I had a real nice time tonight, despite the mix-up with Becky. My friends all like you a lot. Like me." Maddy walked arm in arm with him to the door. He hugged her close.

"Sorry about the ice cream melting. Can we have strawberry next time?" She said in a small voice not wanting to look up at him for fear he'd say, no, there'd be no next time.

"Sure." He lifted her chin again, "Strawberry it is. Now be sure and lock everything up tight after I leave, Miss Independence."

She nodded and he opened the door and started out. He paused, then in one natural move he swept her into his arms and kissed her passionately. Relieved to feel him close to her again, Maddy didn't resist. She kissed him back.

"Strawberry." He murmured and walked out the door. She watched until he drove away.

"Strawberry." She whispered softly to herself.

In the morning, Maddy faced the fact she was going to have to go grocery shopping. She really hated to grocery shop, just more decisions to make. But, she liked to eat, so she couldn't hold off any longer.

The automatic doors parted and a young, carryout boy with a bright smile was the first thing she saw.

"Hi, Maddy," he said cheerfully as he put groceries in a sack for a customer. Dressed in a high school jacket, he took his job seriously. Tommy was taller than Maddy, fresh-faced with brown hair and an infectious grin. The very first time she'd run into the store for garbage bags, he spoke to her right away like they'd been friends for years.

"Hey there, Tommy, how are you doing?" Maddy waved and grabbed a cart. He waved back enthusiastically.

Maddy had learned from Aunt Polly that Tommy often did odd jobs for her aunt and was the town's unofficial mascot at high school. Everyone in town loved Tommy. From the high school jocks to the senior citizens, he was just one of those neat kids who had a heart of gold. He wasn't retarded, just a little slow, the checker had explained carefully out of earshot. It was obvious she and others were very protective of the friendly kid. Charmed immediately by his honesty and natural friendliness, Maddy and he became good buddies.

Maddy filled her cart with all kinds of groceries. It was obvious she was out of everything. The bill was massive but Tommy sacked everything neatly and in no time led the way out to her car.

"Say, Tommy, I hear you used to help my aunt out around her place, would you like to do the same for me? I sure could use the help. I'd pay you, of course."

"Sure, I would." He said without hesitation, "I have to ask my folks, but I'm pretty sure they'll say okay." He looked excited and pleased.

"Good. Let me know. Maybe you could start Saturday. My lawn's growing like a weed patch." She gave him a wide smile.

Aunt Polly sat rocking on Maddy's front porch as she pulled up.

"Hi. Got tired of TV dinners and mooching off of you so I did some major grocery shopping. What's new?"

"Not much. I thought we might finish upstairs. I'm determined to find that missing jewelry. Speaking of which, Leland stopped by. Said to tell you he had a prospective buyer for the house here. He'll stop back."

Aunt Polly glanced at Maddy who was quietly pulling groceries out of the vehicle, a chagrined look on her face.

"I didn't know you were going to put it on the market?"

"To tell you the truth, Aunt Polly, I haven't really made up my mind. I'm sorry I never said anything though. Jack Drake mentioned it, and I guess Leland took the bull by the horns. I'll take care of it."

"I have to tell you, I had to bite my tongue not to say anything about your aunt's jewelry and those fancy books."

Sighing, Maddy nodded patiently, carrying the last of the sacks to the kitchen. "But I did tell him not to rush you about this here house. You got time, don't you? To make up your mind, I mean." Peering at her young friend, Aunt Polly just asked her, "You think you know what you want to do?"

"Funny you should ask that, Aunt Polly." Maddy folded the empty brown sacks and closed the cupboards. "I got a call from my friend in Chicago last night. It was really good to hear from her." Aunt Polly's face fell and she eased back into the wooden rocker in the kitchen. "But, you know, the longer I talked to her, the less I wanted to leave. The longer I'm here," she looked around and smiled, "this feels more like home to me than Chicago ever did."

"Oh, I was hoping you'd feel that way. I know, I know, I won't get my hopes up totally. You need to make up your own mind, but seeing you here, how you look and act like you been born and raised in Nielsen." The old woman's eyes lit up immediately.

"Well, I do feel comfortable here most of the time. And, I didn't get the promotion, and that had a little to do with it. Just don't say anything to anyone, I still have some things to work through, but it won't be a rash decision. Leland will just have to wait until I'm ready to sell this house."

"Good for you." Aunt Polly slapped her thigh gleefully. "That's good enough for me. You use your own instincts, especially with Leland. Besides, houses aren't selling that good in small towns. And I got to tell you, I'm getting awful fond of you, too."

"That's nice to hear, Aunt Polly. Everyone has made me feel welcome. Another thing is, I need to find a job if I decide to stay. My inheritance won't last forever."

"Well, at my age I've learned not to worry and fuss, it doesn't help. Things will work out the way they're supposed to work out." Giving herself a boost out of the rocking chair she rubbed her hands together. "Let's get to work if you're done stashing all your loot from the grocery store."

Maddy led the way upstairs and Aunt Polly headed for the first of four bedrooms. Each one held a simple bed, chest of drawers, nightstand and a small table or desk with a chair. An antique washstand with a beautiful pitcher and basin stood in a corner of each room also. The hardwood floors lay under a coating of dust, and rag and braided throw rugs were scattered liberally about.

A bathroom at the end of the hall held another claw foot bathtub adorned with bronze fixtures and cherubs. The hallway itself boasted several original oil paintings of her aunt's with lighting tracts illuminating them, and the last door by the bathroom led upstairs into the attic. The light fixture didn't work there so they decided to wait for Alec to check it on his day off.

"I hate dark, creepy places like this attic, Aunt Polly." Maddy peered up in the darkness and shivered. "I checked, there's a lot of stuff up there."

They left that for Saturday and began on the rooms with added fervor. Domestic chores never were Maddy's favorite, ranking right up with grocery shopping. But, with Aunt Polly helping it went smoothly and as exhausted as she felt, it was a job well done. Everything sparkled by the end of the day.

"Aunt Polly, you're a whirlwind when it comes to cleaning. Now, I don't want you to overdo it. I wonder," Maddy said absently as they finished putting clean sheets and a blanket on the last bed, "why did my aunt keep all these rooms ready to use. Did she have a lot of company?"

"No, not really. But anytime the pastor called with a poor soul who needed bed and board, she'd open up a room. It was the same with emergencies. One family was burned out of their farm home, she put them up. Another time a tornado completely destroyed a family home, she put them all up for a couple weeks." Tucking a neat hospital corner on her side of the bed Aunt Polly smiled reflectively. "Your aunt was a natural caretaker. She was in her glory when the house was full of people and activity. Just wish we'd have found the jewelry and books."

Maddy gathered up the cleaning supplies and they stood back surveying their finished handiwork. Satisfied with their progress they closed the last door just as the doorbell rang.

"Leland." They said in unison and then laughed.

"Well, I'm getting out while the getting's good. You have to talk to him, I don't. See you later." Aunt Polly headed down the hall and out the back door before Maddy could argue.

"Good afternoon, Miss Morris. Did Mrs. Smith tell you I was coming?"

"Yes, I've been expecting you. We definitely have some things to discuss. You certainly look bright and cheerful, Mr. Lancaster, come on in the kitchen, I need to get rid of these cleaning things. We just finished the upstairs."

"Thank you, have a golf game later on today. You sure have made the place sparkle, I must say. It'll go a long way impressing the buyers who want to see the place just as soon as they can."

"To tell you the truth, Mr. Lancaster, I'm not sure I want to sell."

"Oh, call me, Leland, remember. I think we're good enough friends to be on a first name basis." Then her meaning became clear, "You don't want to sell?"

Maddy put the cleaning supplies under the sink, a rueful smile on her face, which she kept Leland from seeing.

Wiping her hands, she took a long time before answering. "Okay, Leland. Truthfully, I'm not sure I want to sell anymore."

"Look, I know the thrill of owning your own place must be exciting, but this," he swung his hand out in front of him, "it's just too much for a young woman. You must think about this more before jumping into it," he said seriously.

Maddy looked at him impatiently, still irritated at his opinion. "No, I told you I would let you know if I did."

"I just mean, you said you'd finished cleaning upstairs, I thought maybe you might have found something."

Maddy shook her head, busy making a pot of coffee.

"No. We've gone through everything with a fine-toothed-comb. Well, except for the attic and the roll top desk in the library. There was a brown attaché wedged behind the desk, it's full of papers but they looked like bills. I'll go through them sometime and let you know."

"Yes, you do that." He rubbed his forehead as if he had a headache.

"Say, Leland, I do have something else I need to ask you."

"Did you know my Aunt had a black jewelry box? Aunt Polly said she'd seen it before and there were some valuable pieces in it. I haven't been able to find it."

Leland's face was blank and he shook his head slowly. "No, can't say as I do. I wasn't familiar with her jewelry and personal stuff. I know she had a red jewelry case, but a black one? It's missing you say? That is strange."

Maddy nodded and didn't relent in her questioning. "Yes, a strand of pearls, a ruby ring, and a diamond broach, oh, and a set of hand bound, leather books embossed in gold, classics I believe. Aunt Polly thought they might even be first editions. Do you know anything about them?"

"It might have been taken in the break-in." Leland suggested. "Mrs. Smith should recall that, she called the deputy. He did show up and investigate, but never found out who broke in. It's not good to have an empty residence. Another reason a single woman shouldn't have a big old place like this."

"I suppose." But Maddy wasn't convinced.

"Good. Good. I hope they're recovered but I doubt it. Now, getting back to the house, I hate to push it, but I do have an interested party that wants to look at the place. I think you ought to show it to them. They're cash buyers who want out of the big city badly. What do you think?"

"I don't know." Maddy was unsure, but a cash buyer in this day and age was rare for anything. Leland's ominous description of the problems of owning a house like this reared up in the back of her mind. This forced her to come to grips with the situation head on and the cash part was temping. She realized she must make up her mind, and soon.

"Look, if you're still not certain, why not let me just show the place once. If you like their offer, good, if not, you don't have to accept it." Leland stood up and shrugged. The coffee pot gave a loud burp and Maddy poured two cups and sat down, thinking. Leland walked around gazing out the windows, sipping his coffee quietly.

"I tell you, Maddy, there's a lot more work to a place like this than you realize, and for a young woman alone? Why, look at the lawn, it's dry and overgrown and the flower bed needs so much work."

"That's the next thing I was going to start now that the house cleaning is done." Maddy defended herself, but his list of all the chores waiting to be done was beginning to exhaust her.

"As I came in I noticed the outside is due for a coat of paint and a shutter's hanging. I know there are rooms inside that need some major work too."

"Yes, that's all true." Maddy sighed, recalling a very poor job done of patching water damage in one of the back bedrooms. "I suppose showing it once won't hurt as long as I'm not obligated in any way. Understood?"

"Yes, of course. I'll just need your signature on a form concerning my commission, just in case there is a sale." Leland sighed in relief.

"Well, it's just a formality," he said, but when she glared

at him he tucked the papers back in his bright sports coat. Trailing behind her as she got up he smiled. "I'll call before we come."

"Fine." Maddy opened the door, eager for him to go. But now that he had basically what he wanted he wasn't in any hurry to leave. He acted as cheerful as his sunny yellow coat.

"You say you haven't done the attic yet?"

Maddy nodded and absently rubbed her tired eyes.

"I don't know. Mostly furniture from the quick look I took. The light doesn't work so Alec is coming Saturday to check it."

Maddy leaned against the door in relief when he left, wondering if she had done the right thing in allowing him to show the house, even once. She had a feeling she should have said no, but the die was cast.

"I don't know, Maddy, I don't trust him." Aunt Polly said as she chewed thoughtfully on the steak and salad Maddy fixed for supper that night. Alec needed a rain check since he had to work but said he'd stop by later. After her little session with Leland, Maddy needed someone to talk to.

"I know you don't trust him. After today, I don't think I trust him either, but I don't know why. I thought I'd better see if anyone would be interested in a serious offer on the house, just in case. Cash sales are pretty rare."

Sitting in the cozy kitchen Maddy felt warm and secure as the rays of the setting sun cast a golden glow over the whole back yard. Food tasted better, she slept sounder and got up feeling excited about each new day since arriving in Nielsen. On her best day in Chicago she had never felt like this.

She kept putting off buying another cell phone, relying on the landline. Marie's phone call plagued her. It sounded as if Larry was trying to find out what was going on through her friend.

"You know, Aunt Polly, this trip has been healing for me. Things that had been in the background and puzzling, now are making sense. I've wondered so much about why things were the way they were with my family, now I'm beginning to understand a little."

"You look like you got the weight of the world on your shoulders, honey."

"I feel like it sometimes. In Chicago, it all seemed to run together, work, home, sleep, eat, and work again. I mean, look at that sunset. I've never taken the time to really see a sunset like that before, it's breathtaking." Maddy stood at the chipped porcelain sink and nodded outside. The purple and pink sky with white slashes of clouds broke through the last rays of the sun.

Aunt Polly had tied one of Aunt Madeline's aprons around her ample waist to protect her cotton housedress while finishing up the dishes.

"I know. I never get tired of the view anywhere around here, either." Folding the damp towel, she hung it on a towel rack and wandered outside with Maddy. They walked among the overgrown garden that bloomed brightly despite the weeds.

"Look, there's hollyhock back there. You say Tommy is coming over to do the lawn tomorrow?" Aunt Polly slapped at a mosquito and frowned at Maddy's bare feet. "You're going to step on something, young lady. Better get shoes on those feet." Her gentle reproach was music to Maddy's ears, someone cared again. She slipped an arm around her friend as they followed the stone steps to the adjoining gate.

"I'm going right back inside when you leave."

"Well, I'm leaving now. I'm beat. Since Alec is coming over tomorrow, I'm sleeping in. If you guys need anything just call." Aunt Polly yawned and opened the white picket gate.

"Aunt Polly?" The old woman paused, looking over her shoulder, pulling her favorite crocheted shawl around her.

"I think I've made up my mind to stay, not sell. I still have to figure out if I can afford it, but this..." she swung her arm wide to include the house and yard and sunset, "this is what living should be like. I really do love it here." Maddy swallowed a lump in her throat. Saying it out loud was emotional.

"Shoot. If one good sunset was all it took, I wish I'd drug you out in the yard before. But, you have to listen to your heart and decide in your own good time. Good night, my dear. Lock up tight and sleep well."

Maddy nodded and waved, retreating on the cool stones up to her own back door, she went in and pulled the portable TV out and picked up the daily paper. The routine made her feel like an honest-to-goodness citizen of Nielsen. Even the local newscaster was beginning to look and sound familiar.

She slept well most of the night. Dreams faded in and out of her memory, scary things, unknown and lost things she couldn't understand. As she hugged her pillow after waking up breathless from something that frightened her, Maddy could hardly wait to tell Alec about her decision.

That thought intimidated her a little too, more than the bad dreams. He was a big part of the decision, whether she wanted to admit it or not. What if, *they,* didn't work out? What was it that she was worried about? Loving him, she guessed. Did she? There was always that matter of trust.

Chapter 9

Saturday mornings in Chicago Maddy usually slept-in. But this glorious morning she woke up instantly, showered and anticipated Alec's arrival. She slipped on jean shorts and a cheery, red-checked gingham blouse she felt would be cool and just right for cleaning an attic full of dust and cobwebs.

"Good morning. Is anybody up yet?" Alec tapped on the back screen door, which was locked.

"Hi, come on in." She said smiling as she unlocked the door, "The OJ is frozen, but I just whipped up a batch of muffins, and the coffee is perking. How's that for domestic prowess?" Yanking off the apron Aunt Polly wore yesterday, Maddy held open the door. "Any offer to help when it comes to dark, scary places full of spiders, deserves breakfast as well as my undying thanks."

"Hey, who said anything about scary places? All I said was I'd help you get the lights working in the attic." Alec joked.

He looked great in washed-off jeans and a red Nebraska tee shirt that accented his physique.

"I know. But, if you look up that dark stairway to the attic, it's scary. And I'll be the first to admit that I also hate spiders. How was your day yesterday?" She pointed to a chair and sat down across from him.

"Tiring, I had to go to Lincoln. Wish you could have been with me. It was a long ride home alone." Winking he took a bite of one of her muffins and chewed vigorously.

"Sorry you were all alone. However, Aunt Polly and I finished the whole upstairs, hope you're impressed. It looks great too."

"Bet that's a relief. Did you find any of the mysterious missing jewels?" He wiggled his eyebrows and kept eating.

"Unfortunately, no," she said, lost in thought.

"It's good to get the place cleaned up, what with it being for sale and all." He got up and poured coffee for them both, keeping his back to her. "When did you decide to sell out?" He asked stiffly.

"Sell?" Maddy looked incredulously at him. "Come on. Whatever gave you that idea?" She licked the butter from her fingers. Would he be surprised when she told him she was going to stay.

"Well, the FOR SALE sign in the front yard is usually a good indication." He plopped the coffee mugs down on the table and looked accusingly at her, his blue eyes probed hers.

"Alec, quit it. Quit teasing. I'm not selling." Then she recalled the 'one-time-only' showing Leland had talked her into. Jumping up she ran to the front door and leaning on the porch rail saw what Alec was talking about. Sure enough, a big FOR SALE sign and Leland's realty name right underneath it. *Darn him! Darn that Leland!* Just because he was showing it once he had no business planting a sign out there for all to see. She rubbed her forehead in exasperation.

"I think that means your house is for sale." Following Maddy out, Alec stood next to her and munched on another muffin. He took a big gulp of coffee looking from her to the sign. Wiping his mouth he pointed to it. "Did someone just put that there for no reason?"

"There's a perfectly good explanation, Alec." She began.

"I suppose." Alec didn't sound convinced and walked back into the house. Maddy could have ripped the metal sign in two with her bare hands, she was so angry.

"Alec, I was so excited about telling you something first, I forgot all about Leland and this deal. Why are you acting so funny about it? I'll take the sign down."

Maddy was angry with Leland but Alec was coming in a close second. He probably wouldn't believe her now so she let her temper get the better of her.

"Hey, look. If you don't believe me and you don't want to stay and help, please don't feel obligated." Maddy felt he was overreacting. Maybe her instincts about not getting involved with him had been right. This was just too hard on her heart.

"No, I said I'd help you today. I just thought you might have told me first rather than let me see a sign on your front lawn, is all. I told you I've gotten used to having you around." Picking up the flashlight and broom he started for the stairs with her trailing behind holding the dust mop and trash bags.

"Alec, will you slow down a minute? It may interest you to know I told Aunt Polly last night I decided to stay, although I'm having a few reservations about it now. I only let Leland show the house to one couple to get him off my back. Not that it's any of your business. I have an important decision to make concerning my life, mister. I have a good job back in Chicago and dear friends, with goofy names, true. But I care about them." She didn't tell him she felt a lot closer to the friends she'd made in Nielsen lately. But he had eyes, couldn't he see that?

"Fine. Of course you do." He said over his shoulder and continued upstairs.

"Fine." Maddy mimicked, as she stomped up the last few steps and walked past him to hold the door to the attic open. "Be careful, Alec." It was an innocent statement but he glared back at her, switching the flashlight on in her face, making her squint.

"Oops, sorry. There, it works now." Chuckling, he ducked from a swing she took at him and his clowning.

"Great. Now I'll see spots before my eyes for the next hour." She grouched at him.

"Look at it this way, you won't be able to see any of that scary stuff." He was enjoying this.

"Shut up and don't electrocute yourself, it'll detract from the sale of the house and Leland will never forgive you."

"Don't worry about me. You're sure feisty so early in the morning. Maybe I ought to just lock you in here. Hey, there's an old mattress in here."

"Only in your dreams, Buster. And I'm feisty, as you put it, when people are so darned stubborn." Maddy retorted but then said 'Bless You' when he sneezed. Hesitantly they went in further, the flashlight making a dull little splash of light.

"What else do you see?" She whispered and he chuckled.

"What are you whispering about?" He said in amusement and she couldn't help but laugh.

"I'm a librarian. I'm always telling people to whisper." She countered.

A big, long cobweb draped over her and she fought with it, bumping into him. "I don't know. It just seems you should whisper in here, is all."

At that rationale Alec laughed out loud and promptly bumped his head on a swinging light bulb.

"Ow, here's the light fixture, such as it is. If it wasn't broken then it probably is now. Let me check it, hand me a light bulb."

Maddy gave him a new bulb and heard the twisting sound as the old one went out and the replacement went in. Suddenly light filled the room and Alec snapped his flashlight off. He looked quite pleased with himself.

"There. That's better. Just a burned out bulb is all. Add a new light bulb and it's as good as new."

"No thanks to your hard head, deputy." She moved past him and looked around. Everything was dusty. A dirty window covered by an even dirtier curtain stood high up on the peak of the roof, filtering any sunlight that tried to get in. Gingerly Maddy pushed the curtain aside, but could see little.

Old furniture, boxes and two big steamer trunks caught her eye. A full-length mirror on a swivel stared back at them. A dress form stood silently with other old attic regulars. A wire birdcage and empty picture frames hung haphazardly around.

"See anything interesting?" Alec dusted off his hands.

"Check the bureau first and see if anything is in the drawers like papers or books. Otherwise, this just looks like a dusty old attic to me." She went to the steamer trunk.

Alec saluted and opened the top drawer, "As you wish." Rummaging through old clothes he called out after a few minutes. "Maddy, I found something. A book, I think. It looks old. Do you want it?"

"Yes." Maddy stumbled over boxes to get at it. "Look. It says Diary on the front. That's great. Is there anything more?"

Frowning, he handed the book to her and rummaged through the rest of the drawers. "No. That's it for the dresser. The diary is locked. Do you want me to pry it open?"

"No, there's a whole bunch of keys I found downstairs, we'll try them first before we break it. What a find."

Eyes sparkling she clutched the book to her chest and looked excitedly at Alec. "This would make good reading curled up in front of the fire this winter, if I could wait that long to read it, which I can't."

"That sounds like you are serious about staying. Nebraska winters can be pretty long." Alec dropped the last of the rotten clothes in a trash bag and turned to look at Maddy. She stood in the swaying light of the naked light bulb, her face smudged, and a cobweb in her shiny copper-colored hair. The genuine happy look she gave him, her face turned up to him so sweetly, full, red lips, eyes the color of emeralds. At that moment it took his breath away.

"Are you kidding? I live in Chicago. Now that's a tough winter place. I know what winter is like. I told you I was serious, but you're so hardheaded about one showing of the house, you don't even notice how serious I am." Leaning against the old bureau, she nodded smugly.

"So then, I don't have to lock you up here to keep you from going back to Chicago?" He grinned mischievously and leaned on the opposite side of the bureau, staring intently at her.

"No. Unless Leland gets a big offer I can't refuse." Returning the teasing she rested her chin on her hand.

"You know where Leland can go as far as I'm concerned. All I need is something to eat once in a while, a little rest now and then, and a beautiful woman to kiss."

Edging around the bureau, he stepped carefully to avoid the garbage bags full of junk, keeping a wary eye on Maddy who tempted him by just being around him.

"You want it in that order?" She shook her head. "Now Alec, we're not done up here, yet. Come on. Don't goof around." Laughing and giggling, they put all arguments aside and faced each other until Maddy tripped and they collapsed on the old fainting couch. A puff of dust went up around them and instead of kisses, they came up coughing. He threw back his head and laughed as they dusted each other off.

"Oh, brother," she sputtered, "if you're not allergic to dust before, you will be now. This is awful."

"It's awful fun." He quipped, wiping a cobweb from her hair. He dusted down her arms and let his hands settle on her waist, pulling her close.

"I'm going to feel this grit until I take a shower. And you're even worse."

"I can't seem to get enough of you, Madeline Morris. I don't think, no, I'm quite sure I've never felt like this before, unless it was fifteen years ago when I kissed you right after the Homecoming Dance."

"It's probably the dust, Alec. I feel a little strange myself." Maddy's hands gripped his upper arms with a strength she didn't know she had. His muscles tightened in response and refused to relax.

"Alec, don't say that. Not yet. It takes time, and I don't want you to say what you think I want to hear. Not yet, I don't know where this is going to lead us."

"I know where I hope it leads us." He said and kissed her again, his breath caressing her face tenderly, his fingers running through her silky hair.

"I hate it when the situation calls for 'understanding,' it usually means 'waiting.'" Groaning, he closed his eyes and buried his face in her hair.

"If being understanding will keep you here, then I'll do it. But, it's not going to be easy, I'm sure."

That wasn't much for him to ask, she thought. Her heart gave a little lurch. Larry would never have reacted like that. Alec's unselfishness lifted a great weight from her shoulders.

"Okay, maybe some time later. Not now, if you don't mind. I don't want anything to spoil the way I feel right now. So, come on. I'm dying to get into those old trunks next."

"Okay, come on." Giving her a hand up he wiggled his eyebrows menacingly at her, making Maddy laugh.

Opening the heavy trunk lid revealed nothing but more old clothes and some newspapers in one. The period clothing Maddy decided to keep since they were in better condition from being in the trunk. The second trunk was beautiful with dull brass hinges and rich leather. Inside, more clothes and she felt her heart race. Alec lifted the heavy tray and underneath was several bundles of letters tucked away. One bunch was tied with a faded red ribbon and the others were tied with plain string.

"Oh, my goodness, Alec, look." Maddy whispered excitedly, holding up the two packets of yellowed letters.

"There you go with the whispering again. Is that what

you're looking for?" Rocking back on his heels he paused and squinted.

"I don't know, but they've got to be as good as the diary. Do you see any documents, like stock certificates or anything?"

"When I read these it will be like seeing what great Aunt Madeline thought and felt. See, the ones with the red ribbon must be from her husband." Eyes wide, she stared from the letters to Alec excitedly. "The others, I don't know. There are initials A.C. in the return addresses. I can't tell until we get in some good light, they're so faded."

"Well, at least it's something." Alec said as he looked through the rest of the trunk but found nothing else.

"Come on. I can hardly wait to get downstairs and see what they say." Standing up, she was startled when the attic door slammed shut with a loud bang.

"What was that?" Alec said, frowning. The loud slam sent the slender cord with the light bulb swaying back and forth.

"Could that have been the wind?" Maddy asked in a small voice, clutching the letters and diary tightly.

"What wind, in an attic?" He replied tersely.

"It was just a suggestion. Besides, what else could have caused it?" They both made their way to the attic door. It was shut tight as if were locked.

"Alec, can you get it open? I know we didn't lock it when we came in. Is it stuck?"

"Well, it's stuck good. Could someone have locked us in?"

"Who would lock us in? That's silly, it must have slammed shut accidentally and then locked, didn't it?" Maddy was reaching for explanations as she stood closely behind Alec.

"If it slammed shut accidentally, someone had to lock it, Maddy. You didn't happen to bring any of those keys up you were talking about, did you?" She shook her head.

"I haven't gotten that far, finding out which keys go where. Do you have your cell phone?"

"No. What a time to leave it in the car." He belittled himself.

She went over to the dirty window and used the bottom of the curtain to wipe the grime off and was shocked to see movement below in her yard.

"Alec! Come here. Look! There's a strange man in grubby clothes running down the sidewalk away from the house."

Maddy pulled him closer to the window and pointed to the little clean circle she'd rubbed on the dirty window.

"Do you know him?" They watched the young man with long, stringy hair trying to hide something under his arm as he ran away. "What's that he's got in his hands?"

"Alec, he's got the leather briefcase, my Aunt's leather briefcase. Aunt Polly and I found it stuffed behind the old desk in the library. How could he know about that? Alec, we've got to stop him, maybe the missing bonds are in there."

"Well, it would help if we could get out of here," Alec said in frustration.

"It's locked remember? Besides, he just jumped into a van and drove off. We'll never catch them now." Alec joined her at the door, testing the hinges and finally leaning against it. Agitated Maddy flailed away at the door until he pulled her down to sit next to him.

"Maddy, settle down, I don't think it's locked, I think it's jammed or blocked from the outside. We can't move it. What was in that briefcase, anyway?"

"I'm not sure. Papers, I think old receipts. I hadn't had time to look at them closely. We found the case when we were cleaning and it didn't look like much more than bills and things so I thought I'd look them over later. I can't imagine anyone taking old papers, for goodness sakes. Oh, Alec, the briefcase was in my bedroom, I hope he didn't take my purse and cash. Why would anyone steal old papers unless they knew what they were?"

"Like what?" Alec said uneasily.

"Like old stock certificates that my aunt had misplaced. But how would anyone know about that particular briefcase?"

"That's a good question, Maddy. Come on, we have to get out of here somehow. I've got to call the office and get an APB out on the van. I wish I could have gotten the license plate number."

They looked out the window once more hoping to see someone passing by they could call to, but no one was around. Alec went back to work on the door while Maddy sat on the window ledge holding the letters and diary.

"You're just raising more dust with all that activity, Alec."

"Okay, we're going to have to break out this window, then and signal for help. Stand back." Just then she saw a familiar sight below. It was Tommy. Tommy the boy from the grocery store was coming to mow the lawn, she'd forgotten. He rode up on his ten-speed bike and leaned it against the garage, looking around. Yelling and screaming, they pounded on the window and managed to raise it a crack. Looking up, Tommy squinted into the sun and finally waved back.

"Tommy! Tommy! Up here, we're stuck. Come up stairs

and let us out!" Maddy yelled. He nodded and they waited patiently, the sounds of something heavy scraped against the door and then it opened.

"Hi, you guys. What are you doing locked in the attic?" Tommy stood grinning at them.

"Tommy, you're a lifesaver." Alec rushed past him, patting his arm.

"I am? Cool." Tommy's grin grew. Maddy agreed and ushered him down behind Alec. A heavy chair was beside the door, it had been propped under the door knob locking them in. This was no accident.

"How'd you get the chair under the doorknob and still be inside, Maddy?" Tommy asked innocently. Suddenly another thought hit her. What if Tommy had come over earlier and confronted the strange man? The thought of anyone hurting him sickened her.

"Oh, it was kind of a game, Tommy. Someone tricked us, is all. But it wasn't very nice. Just forget it and get started on the lawn, okay? You know where the mower is?"

"Yeah, I used the same one for Miss Madeline." The sounds of the mower buzzing softly in the distance could be heard a few minutes later.

"Maddy, check and see if anything else is missing besides the briefcase." Alec said in a professional tone.

After checking to make sure no one else was in the house, he picked up the phone and called his office. Maddy was still frightened at the brazenness of the burglar.

"He went through things, I can see that. But I don't think he took anything else. Oh, my goodness." Maddy looked in her bedroom. The dresser drawers hung with clothes draped over them, her suitcases were thrown about the room with linings ripped out. The dressing table drawers lay on the bed upside down, books, papers and even the mattress had been pulled off. Aghast, Maddy looked around, stepping gingerly around the shambles in shock.

The little red costume jewelry box was empty and open and she bent to pick it up.

"Don't touch anything." Alec barked and her hand stopped in mid-air. "I called the office. They'll be right over. Maybe we'll get lucky and there will be some fingerprints." She nodded and stepped back, rubbing her arms. Suddenly she felt very cold.

"I don't think anything else is missing, but I'm not sure. I found my purse, cash and credit cards are gone. I don't know, Alec, there could be more missing."

"Well, he definitely was looking for something in particular. But I don't think he found it. I think he tried to make it look like he was after the money." Alec gave her a reassuring look, cradling the phone on his shoulder.

The rest of the afternoon the officers spent going through her home, filing reports and forms, talking with both of them. Tommy enjoyed all the excitement and Aunt Polly came running over with a towel wrapped around her freshly washed head to see what was wrong. Even the weather grew unfriendly, thick and muggy, clouds boiled up over the horizon as a storm brewed.

"I've got to go to the office for a little while." Alec tapped his notebook on his hand and looked soberly at her. "I sure wish I knew what they wanted. Those missing stock certificates are the best bet. Nobody could have known about the diary and letters, but who could have known about them?"

"I don't know. But, it's pretty brazen. It's like they waited for us to go up to the attic, snuck up and barricaded the door. That was awful risky, and in broad daylight too. Don't make sense." Alec wasn't convinced. "Are you going to be all right? You look a little pale." His strong fingers massaged her neck and shoulder lightly.

"I'm okay. Just a little spooked. When can I get in my bedroom and disinfect after that creep touched everything."

"Soon as they all clear out. I know I sound like a broken record but I sure hate leaving you alone. Would you want to come to the office with me?"

"Thanks but, I'm not running." Maddy said firmly.

"I forgot. You're Miss Independence." He said drily.

"I'll be here, Alec." Tommy spoke up, his innocent face intent. "Nobody will bother Maddy when I'm here."

Maddy put an arm around Tommy's shoulder and squeezed it. "Hey, don't worry. I'll lock up after you leave."

"Okay, but I'll have a patrol car drive by later. If anything happens, call me. Maybe you should think about staying somewhere else tonight. Seriously, this is not just a prank. I've got a spare room."

"I'll just bet you do. But no, nobody's going run me out of my home now that I've finally got one. I told you that. But thanks for the offer."

He sighed and shrugged but he wasn't convinced.

Alec left with an uneasiness he couldn't describe. Right now, Maddy seemed very vulnerable. He'd been in law enforcement for a while and enjoyed the lack of serious crime in the small town he'd grown up in. He'd been involved in some dangerous situations before, but nothing that racked up the doubt and fears he was beginning to have with this.

Coupled with Maddy being so independent it worried him even more.

He'd gone on with his life after his divorce with the attitude that he'd never get involved again. That all went out the window when Maddy came back to town. He'd thought of her often over the years, she'd been his girl since the first time they'd met in junior high. When she left he was crushed, but life went on. Only weeks before she blew back into Nielsen, he stood with a beer in one hand and Bubba at his side and vowed he would never get tangled up seriously with any woman again. Well, so much for that.

There was an aura around the independent, strong-willed little redhead that captivated him, as if he'd just been waiting for her to return. Maddy was right to proceed slowly, but the ease with which he felt drawn to her blocked out his caution. She was back and everything felt right. At night he prayed no one from Chicago would be able to pull her away. The whole world took on a different light when she was beside him, with her on his side he could do anything. His job now was to keep her safe, no one must hurt her. He'd see to that.

After Alec left, Maddy hesitantly looked up and down the deserted street. Tommy worked hard till suppertime and then went home. She was just putting the last few branches on the brush pile when Aunt Polly walked over.

"The yard looks as good as the inside of the house now. How about calling it a day?"

"Yeah, that Tommy is a hard worker. He's going to keep on helping me."

"I'm glad you trimmed up the lilacs, they were about taking over the porch."

"Alec suggested that. He said the overgrown stuff was a

good place to hide someone." Maddy gave a shiver and they walked to the porch to rest.

"How are you doing after all the commotion today, my dear?"

"You know, it was funny, like it was happening to someone else, Aunt Polly. I don't know if I could even identify this guy, I only saw him from behind."

"It's plain awful. A body isn't safe in your own home any more." Aunt Polly fussed and pushed the wicker rocker back and forth with her foot.

"I know. I always lock up tight at night, but during the day when I'm around I'm not as careful. Guess things aren't as different from Chicago after all."

"I just can't figure it out. It's too much of a coincidence. Out of all the stuff in my room, they take that tacky old briefcase full of ancient papers. I just wish we'd looked more carefully at them. Maybe they could have told us where the stock certificates are. Now someone else might find them."

"Who would know that?"

Smacking her forehead, Maddy jumped up and began pacing. "Only Leland and Jack Drake know about them besides us. Jeez, I told him about the briefcase, too. Aunt Polly, it had to be him."

"Or someone he hired. Never did trust him, I told you that. You ought to go right over and confront him."

"I can't do that, I don't have any proof." She flopped back down, "Rats. I can't go off half-cocked as Alec would say. It could make things worse. It could be a coincidence." Aunt Polly snorted and looked away.

"Not likely. I see Leland didn't waste any time getting that sign up on your front lawn. When are you going to take that thing down? People have been calling me all morning about it, asking if you were leaving. I told them no."

"I don't think Alec even believed me, that's what made me so mad."

"Oh, he'll settle down, he's high spirited is all, one to get things done right and proper. Lately he's been even more stubborn. I think he's worried about you. I don't know, he can be a hard one to figure sometimes."

A crash of thunder made them both jump and the rain came down in torrents. The wind gusts made Aunt Polly and Maddy scramble for indoors. Shaking off the damp chill, they were making supper when Alec burst in, soaking wet and hungry.

"Hello everyone, it's a hurricane out there tonight."

"You didn't have to come right over," Maddy scolded, noticing his tired eyes. She knew he and Aunt Polly didn't want her to be alone after the break in. As much as she didn't want them to worry, she felt a deeper affection for them both for doing it.

After supper, Alec walked Aunt Polly home while Maddy cleaned up the kitchen and tried to find the key to unlock the mysterious diary.

"Maddy, I still think you should stay somewhere else tonight." Alec had come in the back door so quietly she hadn't even heard him. He shook off the rain and sat down at the kitchen table beside her.

"No, I'll be fine. Besides, who but a duck would be out in weather like this?"

"I know but, and I'm asking as a deputy sheriff, Maddy, to let me stay over. I'll take the couch and be just fine."

"Didn't you just tell us at supper you have to work again early tomorrow morning? Besides, if we should happen to bump into each other during the night, I don't know what would happen."

"That's your fault for kissing so well." He took her hand and squeezed it gently.

"You're not such a bad kisser yourself. But, no, I'm not going to worry about you being overtired just because you think I'm scared."

"What if they come back?" He looked seriously at her.

"They're not likely to, you said so yourself. I've got a phone, a bat under the bed and you've got cars cruising by all night. I'll be fine. I don't want you sitting up all night for nothing and that's final."

Sitting in his truck after they said their good-nights, Alec watched and thought about his next move. There was no evidence against anyone at this point. As the rain started again he knew he'd just have to watch and wait. He ran a hand through his hair.

Whether they meant to or not, the thought of anyone trying to hurt Maddy, enraged him. He drove around the block and parked where he could see Maddy's house, but she couldn't see him. He sat patiently with a loving vigilance until the early morning hours.

Chapter 10

After Alec left, Maddy carefully double-checked all the doors and windows. *Why is it when it gets dark you're not nearly as brave as in the daytime,* she wondered to herself. Getting a glass of milk and some cookies, she curled up in bed and pulled the diary and letters out.

Even though she didn't like to admit it, at first she was uneasy alone in the house after having a stranger there. When everyone left Aunt Polly had helped her strip the bed and put fresh sheets on. Anywhere the burglar might have touched was thoroughly cleaned. Everything was locked up tightly, so she sighed and tried to settle in.

Only the fascination with what was in the letters and diary kept her attention. Luckily one of the tiny keys on a key chain fit the lock and her Aunt Madeline's world was there in her own handwriting.

She opened the thick leather cover almost reverently. The stiff pages were yellowed, but the handwriting was feminine and neat. The diary began the year before her aunt ran away. After reading a few pages, Maddy could tell her Great Aunt Madeline's life had been full of bitterness and anger at the way she was treated.

August 11, 1924

My parents have enrolled me in a Catholic boarding school in upper Chicago. I'm not to call or have contact with anyone from home until Christmas. What hurts is they act like I have no feelings, but I do have a plan.

August 15, 1924

Mother took me shopping today. They want me to have the best of everything except love. They care how I look, but not how I feel. Plan is progressing.

August 20, 1924. School starts in two weeks. I haven't much time. Had another awful fight with father again then Grandmother locked me in my room. I'm leaving as soon as I can.

The next few entries were faded out and illegible. Maddy sat back and contemplated what it must have been like for her aunt. Her Aunt Madeline's spirit and independence were admirable, especially since Maddy knew how formidable great Grandmother Morris could be. She read on and on until her eyes grew heavy.

Glancing at the alarm clock, Maddy yawned. She should try and get some sleep. It was after 1 a.m. already. She put the diary down and touched the letters fondly, anxious to see what they said too. She needed to rest her eyes just for a few moments.

Snuggling under the covers she listened to the wind blowing outside. The cottonwood tree branches tickled the window screens and sent shivers down her spine. Trying to pick up where she left off was impossible. Her eyes refused to stay open. Gathering up the book and letters she tucked them safely under her pillow. The last thing she recalled were shadowy figures dancing and playing on her walls in tune to the wind.

Sunday dawned bright and clear. With Alec having to be on duty Maddy promised to go to church with Aunt Polly, and Leland called and said he planned on showing the house at eleven, the one and only time, Maddy reminded him. So, Aunt Polly invited her over for dinner after church.

Maddy wore a green suit with her Aunt's cameo. When Aunt Polly saw it she nodded in approval. She had traded in her Reeboks for a sturdy pair of low-heeled pumps and a suit.

"Your Aunt would have been so pleased to see you wear that jewelry. It meant a lot to her, just like you did." She said as they walked to church.

The simple fact was Maddy was happy with her decision to stay and belong to something and someone. The small town girl was slowly reappearing, and although the doubts that lingered was more about the decisions she needed to make, they were tempered by moments like this.

"I'm going to break the sad news to poor old Leland right after he shows the house, and, unless they offer me a million dollars cash, I'm staying put."

"I'm going to pray for really poor Looky-Loos today," Aunt Polly said.

"There's no amount of money that could give me the satisfaction I'm feeling right now, Aunt Polly. And, after going over the accounts here and what I have left in Chicago, I think I can make it stretch just fine."

"Well, where there's a will there's a way, my old Granddaddy used to say. If you ever need anything all you have to do is ask."

Maddy patted her arm reassuringly and shook her head.

"That's nice but it won't be necessary, that's why I'm taking so long to see if I can really afford to move here. I'm going to have to find a job eventually, but I'll be okay for a while until I decide what I want to do."

"Well, there's one deputy I know who won't let you starve."

"Now, don't go rushing that either, Aunt Polly. Don't act like you aren't trying to do a little matchmaking. I'm still trying to figure out how I feel about Alec. Oh, that's dumb, I miss him the moment he walks out the door. But it's been such a short time since we met again. I guess I get a little scared when I have to trust someone. Just don't be giving him any more ideas. Things have to move a little slower, I've made too many mistakes in that area of my life."

"Guess that Larry character hurt you pretty bad, huh?" Aunt Polly tucked Maddy's arm in hers as they walked.

"More than a little, but I'm getting over it. I should have never accepted his ring so fast. It probably wasn't even a real diamond, not that that matters. If I love a guy I don't care if I even got a ring. It's hard to admit I made a mistake with him. I thought he was the one, but I couldn't trust him. It's all about trust for me." It was still hard for her to talk about how afraid she was to trust anyone fully, so she shrugged and kept walking.

When they got back from church Leland and his prospective clients were waiting on the front porch for her to let them in. She crossed the lawn and unlocked the door, coming back to sit with Aunt Polly on her porch.

"I hope you put those letters in a safe place." Her neighbor looked over at Maddy's house.

"Don't worry." Maddy patted her purse. "They're not leaving my sight, not after what happened yesterday."

"Good for you, Maddy."

"Here, listen to this one." Settling back in her lawn chair Maddy read from the diary. Aunt Polly rocked as she listened.

September 16, 1929

I finally got a job in a diner, not glamorous but it'll pay the rent. I love being on my own. Heard the family is really angry and talk of disowning me, as if I care. I'm working a lot of nights. Must be careful.

September 30, 1929

I thought I would miss the family but so far, okay. Don't know if the detectives are still looking for me. No one could drag me back now. Not enough money saved yet.

They stopped because Leland and his party were leaving. Looking professional as usual, he wore a sharp navy suit with a red tie and white shirt. They watched as Leland pointed out things on the outside of the house to the people. Maddy and Aunt Polly exchanged worried looks.

"He sure is pushing the positives at your place. You got to give the guy credit, he's a good salesman. Let's just hope not too good, however."

The couple with him seemed to be taking it all in, but from a distance, it was hard to tell how interested they were. They were inside a long time. The woman was young and well dressed, but she kept her arms folded and seemed in a hurry. The man hardly looked at the outside and was first to get in the car. Maddy found it strange they didn't look excited like a young couple should. If she were house hunting she'd be all over the place. They left and Leland came over to Aunt Polly's.

"Well, Leland, your pigeons fly the coop already?"

"Oh, really, Aunt Polly, business is hard enough without any jokes. Where is Miss Maddy?" He seemed a bit out of sorts. When Maddy joined them, the diary and letters were out of sight.

"Hello, Leland, well, what did they have to say?"

"I think they liked it a lot. The roominess impressed them. They wanted a lot of storage so they checked the closets and storage spaces. Pretty good prospects I think." He seemed pleased with himself.

"How much did they offer?"

"Well, they didn't give me a dollar and cents offer just said no more than a hundred thousand." He smiled smugly. Aunt Polly swallowed hard. It was more than the old house was worth.

"That's a pretty good offer. But, Leland, I've decided not to sell."

"It is a good offer. You want to turn it down just like that? You still want to keep that monstrosity?" His voice was incredulous as he looked from one to the other. "What about your job in Chicago? This is a big decision, have you given it ample thought, Maddy? I'm sure your aunt wouldn't want you to saddle yourself with such a responsibility. A hundred thousand is a good price, ask anyone. Aunt Polly, you tell her." He threw his hands up in surrender.

"Well, yes, it is a good price, if you want to sell."

"I give up. You get a good offer and they don't appreciate it." Leland's shoulders slumped in his well-fitting suit.

"Leland. I appreciate your concern, but I've only been here a short time and, believe it or not, it feels like home here."

"Well, it's Nielsen's gain, I guess. You probably wouldn't have liked that couple as neighbors anyway, Aunt Polly. They were rather odd. He'd go off one way and she'd go another. They went through every closet, drawer and cupboard. I could hardly keep up with them." Maddy felt uneasy hearing that. Their actions seemed odd to her too.

"Leland, what was their name?"

"Oh, that's easy. It's almost funny it's so common. It was Smith, Mr. and Mrs. John Smith." He gathered his paperwork and prepared to go.

"Leland? Did you tell anyone that Alec was coming over yesterday?"

"No, don't think so. I told you I would have taken care of it, remember? Oh, wait, I did talk to Jack Drake, he's been wondering how things are going, if the stock certificates have shown up. I told him you haven't found anything yet." He sounded resigned.

"We're trying to find out who locked us in the attic." Maddy watched Leland carefully.

"I can't believe that happened yet. Did Deputy McKay find out anything?" Leland looked at Aunt Polly and then Maddy. They both shook their heads. "Well, I tried my best."

"Yes, I know you did. That's okay. Thanks, Leland."

"Common name, isn't it, Maddy? John Smith." Aunt Polly raised her eyebrows after Leland left.

"It's a very common name. Almost untraceable, wouldn't you say?"

"Well, what do you make of that?" Aunt Polly said as they watched Leland drive away.

"I don't know. He sounded a little suspicious, too." Maddy dropped the curtain with a sigh.

"He would have made a hefty commission on the sale. I was surprised he gave in so easily." Aunt Polly was thoughtful. "I don't know, maybe he does have your well being at heart. Or, maybe he does want a date with you."

"Who wants a date?" Alec still dressed in uniform, his hand poised to knock when Maddy and Aunt Polly started to laugh.

"The man's got more clothes than I do. Plus, he's old enough to be my father, Aunt Polly." Maddy laughed. Even Alec had to join in.

Accepting a cup of coffee he yawned and sat down looking very tired.

"Just thought I'd drop in and tell you there's been no word on our mysterious van or burglar. It's like it dropped off the face of the earth or something. How'd you get along last night?"

"Okay, I think I'll do some more trimming on that tree outside the bedroom window though." She grinned.

"I'll put it on my list. I make a better tree trimmer than a detective right now. It's really frustrating."

"I know. I thought I might be on to something when I remembered I'd told Leland you were coming over to fix the light yesterday. Besides us, he was the only one that knew that." Silence surrounded them, and Maddy decided to kick things up a notch.

"Okay, enough of this. Who wants to accompany me over to my very own front lawn and knock Leland's sign down? My first official act of residence."

"That's the best news I've had all day." Holding out his hand, Alec let Maddy pull him out of his mini-depression. Laughing together they ran over and pushed the gaudy sign back and forth until it fell over.

"It's really mine now." Maddy looked at the fallen sign like the victor of a battle. Alec slipped his hand around her waist.

"Hope I can say the same thing sometime." He looked at Maddy tenderly with eyes that just couldn't get enough of her.

"We just talked about that, deputy. Patience, remember? But just so you know, there's no one else in my life right now." Teasing she ran a finger over his shiny badge.

"Come on in. I'm calling my friends in Chicago right this minute to tell them the news. Boy, are they in for a shock. Maybe you'll get to meet them when they bring my car down. Oh brother, what am I going to do with my apartment? There's a lot to think about." She closed her eyes and rested her head on Alec's broad chest for a moment before they walked in.

Maddy settled in the chair to dial her friend.

"That's strange. No one answers. They knew I was calling. I wonder why they don't answer?"

"Yeah, that would be weird." Alec replied dryly. "Big city people are weird."

Chapter 11

After a busy day of establishing her residence in Nielsen, Maddy stopped by the grocery store to tell Tommy the good news.

"Hey, that's great Miss Morris. I can sure use any work, I'm saving up for a new computer."

"Well, I'll be needing help, Tommy. There's yard work and a couple upstairs bedrooms need to be cleaned up after the rain, there's a bad leak in one of the rooms."

"Yeah, I remember helping Miss Madeline fix that room one time. It's the one with the striped wall paper."

"That's the one. The paper's peeling right off. We're going to have to pull the rest of it off, and then I'll have someone come in and re-plaster the whole thing."

Tommy waved and grinned, "Just let me know when. And, I'll be over on Saturday's to mow."

Driving away, Maddy felt on top of the world. The faces she passed were beginning to look familiar. Her early morning jogs made her familiar to the townspeople too.

Turning on to Main Street, her street, Maddy leaned forward in surprise to see two vehicles parked in her drive.

"What's going on? That's my car." She squealed and flew from the car the minute she'd parked. Four people stood on the porch casually waiting.

"Marie." Maddy squealed excitedly, giving the pretty dark-haired woman a hug and then turned to the others. That's when the shock set in. "Marie?" Maddy said again, only her voice was verging on anger as her eyes met those of a dark haired man. Turning in obvious rebuff, she lightened again seeing the couple who held hands. "Buffy and Skip, how nice."

She could hardly believe her eyes, her dear friends from Chicago had indeed shown up on her doorstep just as her intuition had suggested. "No wonder I couldn't get you on the phone last night. Whose bright idea was this?" She said between laughs and tears. No one claimed responsibility.

Hugging each one in turn, she couldn't ignore the fourth person, a man, as he stepped slowly from the back of the porch. He wore tan Gucci loafers, impeccably pressed brown slacks and a tan silk shirt.

"Hello, Madeline. Remember me, your fiancée?" She froze at the sound of the familiar voice. A ghost from her past was rising before her very eyes. He came over and tried to give her a kiss but she turned her face, and it was merely a peck on the cheek.

"What are you doing here, Larry?" Maddy didn't hide the displeasure in her voice and pulled away. She looked at the others in astonishment, letting her eyes tell them she wasn't pleased. Buffy and Skip shuffled nervously, obviously uncomfortable, but Marie grabbed Larry's arm and Maddy's and tried to pull the three of them together.

"When Larry heard we were coming out to see you, well, I said why not just come along and surprise her. It's just like old times."

Maddy stared at Marie in disbelief and slipped out of her grasp.

With an innocent smile her friend shrugged. "I told you he was asking about you, well, it was perfectly logical to include him." Marie stood there grinning like the Cheshire cat and Maddy could have easily committed murder.

"Don't I at least get a hello and a hug?" His lips drew back in a wide, winsome smile as if nothing was wrong.

"No, Larry, you don't. I'm really surprised you came all the way out here for nothing. It's been a while. I meant to call, as they say, but I've been busy." The words came out icy and she thought she might become physically ill. Her body language said it all, and for a moment everyone was caught up in the melodrama. Stepping back again, she waved for them to follow her.

"Nice place you have here. A little rustic, but I bet you can get a good price for it." Shoving his hands in his pockets and looking around, Larry seemed not to notice or care about her cool reception. He knew Maddy, her weaknesses and strengths and he also knew how to bide his time.

Marie, intent on making it all one big happy family setting, kept her arm linked with Larry's and chattered on, seemingly oblivious to the fact her friend was furious with her.

"I told him you were way out in the sticks and when we picked up your car and decided to deliver it in person; he thought he might be of some help. He knows all about real estate too, he was telling us on the way down." Marie gushed.

Shocked, Maddy remained silent. Marie was talking like an idiot. She knew how Maddy felt about Larry and she allowed this to happen anyway. A wave of shock and determination set upon Maddy and a whole lot of self-confidence at how to handle it.

Skip rolled his eyes and Buffy poked him but Maddy saw it and it only furthered her anger. Looking around blithely, Marie seemed impervious to the daggers Maddy eyes were shooting at her.

"No *FOR SALE* signs up yet? Or did you unload it already? I wish you would have waited so I could help. I know more about real estate than you do." Larry Preston said bluntly. His suave demeanor and slick talk had changed Maddy's opinion before, evidently he thought he could do it again.

"It's what you keep telling me, Larry, about everything. Come on. Why don't we go in and have some lunch everyone." Maddy changed the subject. Opening the door, she stepped back for her guests. Larry smiled disarmingly as he passed, and Marie tripped after him on his heels like a puppy. Maddy yanked her friend back on the porch.

"What do you mean bringing him along? I can't believe you did this! I told you we broke up. He's acting like nothing has changed. Did you give him the ring and note?"

"Of course I did. It didn't seem to matter. Oh, Maddy, lighten up. You know what Larry's like when he gets a challenge. So, you say you're not engaged to the guy anymore, he thinks you still are. You both have to agree. It's not like you're strangers."

"You bet I know him. That's why I broke the engagement. And the emphasis is on we're not engaged anymore. I don't want to be around him. I don't want him here. How could you be so thoughtless?" Maddy's whisper was now a hiss, but Marie simply shrugged and went inside.

While Skip, Buffy and Larry went on a tour of the house, Maddy prepared lunch.

"Maddy, Larry's still in love with you. He isn't seeing anyone else." Marie pouted as she helped make sandwiches.

"Yes, as opposed to when we were really engaged and he was still seeing other women. I understood that perfectly."

"Well, he's like a lost soul. I gave him the ring and your note but he keeps calling to talk. I think he's really sorry, Maddy. He wants you back."

"You have got to be kidding. Larry's only looking out for Larry."

Usually when Marie gave her that puppy-dog look, Maddy would melt and give in. Not this time.

"This is the same man who is working with my relatives against me to get control of my parent's estate. This is the guy who was seeing other women when we were supposed to be engaged, who proposed just to get me to follow along with what he wanted." Her hands trembled as she reached for dinner plates, her fury mounting at both Marie and Larry.

"Oh, Maddy, give him a chance, why don't you." Marie acted as if she were the one in the wrong. "I know he's kind of bossy once in a while, but he knows he made a mistake. We had a long talk on the drive up and you'd be surprised how much he loves you."

"Oh, I'm surprised. Surprised you don't know me any better. My relatives probably threatened his job if he didn't get me back." Maddy said sarcastically.

"Well, that's what I get for trying to fix things. So sue me." Turning on her heel, she flounced past Larry who was standing in the doorway. "Maybe you can get through to her, Larry. I couldn't."

Larry slouched almost gracefully leaning in the doorway, listening. His black hair was windblown and fell casually across his fore head. Icy blue eyes in a slim, angular face appraised her silently. There was no doubt he was a handsome man and he knew it.

"You know Marie is always for the underdog." He looked at Marie's retreating form patronizingly.

"Are you the underdog or me?" Maddy kept busy.

"Ouch, that hurt. Hey, I know this must be a bit awkward, but it isn't over just because you say it is. We are still engaged." Suddenly he was standing right behind her, his hands on each of her arms.

"No, we aren't, and awkward is putting it mildly." Maddy shook his hands loose and pushed past him to get something out of the refrigerator. "You seem to forget I left your ring back in Chicago with a note that I know you got. That was the night before I left. So, we've been officially unengaged for weeks now. I'm sure you can find a girl to give it to, one of many you've been seeing. Or, better yet, ask one of my uncles what to do. You're good at that, too. I just can't believe you'd come all this way and expect to be welcome."

"I know. I got your silly little note. If you don't like the ring, we can get another. Is that it? That's easy enough to fix. But as far as my job, it has nothing to do with it. That's a cold way of looking at it, Maddy. After what we've been through together, the help I gave you. It's just a fight, all couples fight. We make up, and we go on. I can't help what my secretary said. Apparently she has a crush on me."

"Apparently." Maddy wasn't convinced and she wasn't fooled.

"As for dealing with your uncles, we did not plan on disposing of your inheritance. They have helped me with my career. I thought I could help us by investing anything wisely. I didn't think it would hurt anything. Maybe it would help straighten things out between us. Give us a chance to get ahead. Buy the house you've always wanted, have a nice, comfortable life together."

"You couldn't have been more wrong, Larry. It was bad enough you were plotting behind my back with my uncles, now you want me to believe you weren't seeing anyone else?" Maddy slammed the pickle jar down on the table.

"My, my, this isn't the same dear, little Maddy from old Chicago who always was so amiable." Larry Preston had been caught off-guard and reacted with a sneer.

Sauntering over to him, she looked him square in the eye. "It sure isn't."

"Not pulling any punches, huh? Country life must be invigorating." He gave a cynical glance around the old-fashioned kitchen and leaned against a cupboard in a challenging way.

"Sure is. And if you think Marie opinion is going to help you, it won't. Now you've got her under your influence. It's apparent that she doesn't know what I want or need either." Maddy added.

"Do you know what you want or need, Maddy? Seems to me you always had a problem with that. I know that better than anyone." He tried to tuck a piece of hair behind her ear in an intimate gesture, but she slapped his hand away. If he was trying to fluster her, it wasn't working.

"Larry. For the first time in my life, I do know what I want. And believe me, it isn't you. And you should have known better than to try a stunt like this."

"Come on, Maddy, you can't even order from the menu without asking me what I think. You need me, and you know it." Stiffening, his jaw clenched tightly he reached for her but stopped when the others came in for lunch. He backed off temporarily.

While munching on sandwiches, Skip and Buffy raved about the charisma of the old house and their approval pleased Maddy.

"You know, we drove all day and half the night, thirteen hours from doorstep to doorstep to come get you." Buffy chatted aimlessly as she ate.

"Get me? I didn't tell anyone to come and get me. I thought you brought me my car."

"Marie, the last time we talked you said Maddy put the house up for sale and wanted us to come get her." Skip's tone was accusing. Unconcerned, the dark haired girl shrugged and remained silent.

"Skip. What I told Marie is that I hadn't made up my mind yet and I would let her know later in the week. That's why I was so surprised to see you guys."

Skip and Buffy were both upset with Marie at the turn of events. Larry sat back smoking a cigarette, a smug smile on his face as if enjoying the unrest he had caused. Maddy had to put a stop to it for that reason alone.

"Well, never mind. Everything is settled now since I talked to Marie. Are you ready for this? I'm staying. Now put out that cigarette in my new home, Larry." Maddy's voice was clear.

"You've got to be kidding. Staying where, here?" Marie stared incredulously. Larry stubbed his cigarette out, his eyes missing nothing. Skip and Buffy swallowed hard and looked at each other.

"Now, now, Maddy's just trying to rattle us." Larry's voice was smooth as oil.

"Well, she's succeeding." Marie was near tears.

"Maddy, are you really considering staying here?" Buffy said in a quiet voice. "You're not just saying that because you're mad at Marie and Larry?"

"No, I'm not just mad. I've come to love this little town and this house and the people. It's like being in a free fall and when I landed here in Nielsen I just knew it was where I wanted to stay. I feel grounded." Everyone knew she meant every word she said just from the calm look on her face.

She got up to get dessert, the table occupants grew dead quiet. Maddy smiled to herself, I really like being in control for a change.

"You can't mean it." Marie threw her half-eaten sandwich down. "What about your job and apartment, and us? Your whole life is in Chicago not Nebraska."

"I called my supervisor this morning. She won't have any trouble finding a replacement. As far as the apartment is concerned, I'll sublet until I find a buyer." The confidence was building.

"Maddy? About the apartment," Skip and Buffy looked at each other, "we'd lease it from you, maybe even buy it later. I mean, if you're sure. We never thought you'd be happy anywhere but in the big city." Buffy said hesitantly.

"I thought so too, but my life here is so much more. It's simple as that. And if you want the apartment it's yours." Only Larry and Marie were silent and didn't congratulate her. Marie sat sullenly, but Larry kept looking at her as if trying to figure out a way to change her mind.

Maddy stubbornly refused to back down for any of them.

"I'll be okay financially for a while so I'll get by until I find something to do here. Actually I've been thinking this place might make a nice bed and breakfast inn. I have more ideas and a few options." Maddy cut the dessert and passed the plates around.

"Well, we're going to miss you, but if you're really sure, and you look like you are, we'll come back to visit." Buffy said with a renewed enthusiasm.

"What a turn of events." Skip sat back, smiling. Teasing he turned to Larry. "You're awfully quiet, old man, not quite prepared for what happened, huh?"

"She won't go through with it." He said sardonically and turned brooding eyes on Maddy. "It's too much of a change and we all know Maddy hates change."

"You don't know me as well as you think, Larry. But I should thank you. It was your extra curricular activity that made me want something else, something better."

"I wonder though, if Maddy here is telling us everything." Larry's mind was slowly piecing things together.

He leaned forward, resting his chin on his hands, staring intently at Maddy. "It seems when she said she'd come to know the people, she brightened up as if she'd found someone special to know. Am I right?" He found the emotional button and he pushed it.

Surprised, Maddy wished she could push him out of her house right then. He'd turned the tables on her again, like a snake tracking down its prey, he'd figured out an angle to try and use against her.

"Is that true, Maddy? Oh, sorry, if you're not ready to talk about it, it's none of our business." Buffy blurted out then covered her mouth. Maddy patted her hand when Skip glared at her.

"It's okay. I've met a lot of nice people here. But I decided to stay long before I realized there was someone special here." Larry smirked at his correct guess.

"You can't have fallen for someone so quickly." Marie said sarcastically, "And you're certainly not thinking of your friends right now."

Later Maddy took them upstairs to their rooms. Coming down the stairs by herself, she could only shake her head at the way things came to a head. Part of the blame was hers for allowing Marie and Larry to manipulate her the way they did. It had always been easier to give in than fighting with them.

He'd changed to khaki's and a neat white polo shirt and looked quite nice. But this time she wasn't impressed. He followed her into the kitchen where she began arranging cut flowers from her garden.

"So, you're really going to try it." It was a statement not a question. "I just never pictured you as a country girl, or even small town for that matter. As I recall you used to love the bright lights and excitement of the city."

Moving in close behind her, his breath blew softly across her neck when he spoke. Placing a hand on either side of her, he pinned her neatly to the counter.

"I recall a few other things you used to like. Certain things like when we kissed, what we did and said."

"If you want to keep thinking about it, I can't stop you, but I'm not going to marry you and I'm not going to let you talk me out of this. It's over, Larry."

She couldn't stand being so close to him, hearing Larry say things that had been true at one time but no longer. Now his nearness made her queasy. With a well-placed elbow she poked him in the stomach, making him gasp for air and double over as she slipped away from his grasp.

"You are such an egotistical jerk. I can't believe I ever thought I loved you much less could marry you, but it's over."

"It's over when I say it's over." Larry growled rubbing his stomach. "Since becoming a country girl you like to play rough, huh?" A sinister look came over his face. His eyes were dark and nostrils flared.

"If you come near me again, I'll punch your lights out, Larry." She kept the kitchen table between them and looked directly into his dark, angry eyes.

"And if she doesn't, I will." A voice made of steel and ice joined their conversation. Maddy looked up to see Alec's stern face peering at them through the screen door. He must have heard everything.

Larry straightened up. Clenching his teeth he looked at them both with a venomous stare. None too gently, Alec yanked open the screen door, letting it bang shut behind him as he faced his adversary. Skip and Buffy along with Marie entered the room just then.

"Jeez, Larry, what did you do to have the law here already?" Buffy spoke up and Maddy had to grin at the misconception.

"What an entrance, deputy. Your timing is perfect." Maddy spoke under her breath as she moved closer to Alec. "Alec, these are my friends from Chicago. Well, three of them are. This is Buffy and Skip and Marie. That is Larry."

"Oh, he's the one who's leaving?" Alec spoke menacingly and took a step in his direction. Larry gave them all a malevolent look, jerked away from Marie's protective hand on his arm and went upstairs without a word.

Alec turned to the others after Larry left and nodded politely, his familiar grin returning. Skip held out a hand and Alec shook it, which seemed to break the ice.

"Guys, this is Deputy McKay, Alec McKay."

Buffy's eyes were wide and admiring, "Gee, a lawman, Maddy. That's nice and safe." Buffy had a habit of always speaking from the heart and usually without thinking, but no one took offense and even Alec joined in the laughter.

"Well, just for the record. Maddy didn't call. I was just passing by and saw all the cars. She said she wanted me to meet you though." He winked at her. "No time like the present."

Recalling their squabbling over names, Maddy blushed, but was so glad to see him she didn't care. She'd never seen Larry act the way he had, and to be truthful, she'd been a little frightened of him.

"Well, I'll go see how Larry is." Marie gave Alec a stiff nod and disappeared upstairs. A short time later, he and Marie came down with their suitcases and announced they were leaving.

"He asked me to drive back with him. Buffy and Skip can take your rental back and you'll have your own car here. He needs someone. I'm going. No hard feelings, Maddy. I never meant to make trouble, just fix things. Sorry." Shifting the heavy suitcase from one hand to the other, her friend shrugged off Maddy's protests.

"I can't believe this." Skip said to no one in particular.

"He won't be good for her either. Poor Marie, if he sticks around a month, she'll be lucky." Buffy predicted with a sigh and joined Skip in the other room.

The lace curtains swayed briefly in the wind at the abrupt departure. Alec came up behind Maddy, his hands rested on her shoulders in a comforting gesture.

"It's like the end of a friendship when she walked out that door, Alec. Worst part of it is I know she'll get hurt. Larry's a user. He'll use her up and then leave her."

"You tried to warn her, Maddy. Come on. You've still got a couple friends that are staying." He bent down and hugged her from behind. "And you know what? I think I'm going to like that old Skip. And Buffy, she's sure cute."

"Oh, you think so, huh?" She wiggled out of his grasp and slapped at him playfully, "How cute?"

"Not as cute as you."

"Good answer, come on."

"I guess Larry didn't like the room you gave him, Maddy." Skip tied to keep a straight face as they settled down in the living room later.

"Well, I did give him the one that needs repapering." They all laughed and enjoyed easy conversation as they got acquainted. Skip and Buffy were full of wedding plans, and surprisingly, Alec really did seem to enjoy her friends.

"Tell you what, Maddy. We'll have a big old-fashioned barbecue to celebrate your staying and Buffy and Skip's engagement. I'll invite my friends and fire up the grill."

"What do you think about it, guys?" Maddy turned to the couple and they nodded enthusiastically.

"We can have it at my place," Alec offered.

"Oh, no, let's have the party here. It can be a housewarming, too." Maddy said excitedly.

"That's a great idea. We'll have room to set up the volleyball net in your yard." Alec's excitement was infectious. Maddy never had hosted a big party before but it sounded like fun. The afternoon was over too quickly, and Maddy walked Alec to his patrol car.

"Sure you can't stay longer?" She liked to have him around.

"No, wish I could. I traded shifts with a guy at work. But I'm relieved you won't be alone tonight."

"Worry wart, I told you I have a baseball bat under my bed. Actually it's Aunt Polly's, she had an extra one."

"That was lucky for Larry. Hey, I really do have to go to work. Not much else would keep me away, you know that?"

"Something like that, I'm just glad I popped in when I did today. If that guy calls or comes back and bothers you, you know what to do."

Her touch brought him back to the present, and he relaxed and kissed her fingers, folding them into his own.

"What's the matter? Don't you think I handled him pretty good? I thought I did fine." She flexed her arm muscle and tried to look tough.

Alec paused a moment before answering, amusement on his face as he tried to cover a grin.

"Oh, I wasn't worried about you so much. It was poor, old Larry I felt sorry for. That was a good move with the elbow. Looked like it hurt."

He waved at Skip and Buffy and got in his car. Laughing

she shook a fist at him and then waved as he drove away.

"He's quite a guy, Maddy. Much improved from your last boyfriend." Buffy stood on the porch behind her.

"Yes, he is." Maddy hugged herself happily and smiled in agreement. "I never believed I'd find a love anymore until now. But we're not rushing into anything. We're having too much fun getting to know each other again."

"You're playing it smart, girl." Skip interrupted, "Look how Buffy rushed me into marriage."

"Yes, how long have you been going together? Six years. Some rush job." Maddy figured with Buffy agreeing.

"We're in it for the long haul." He bent over and kissed Buffy.

That's what I want, Maddy thought, watching her two friends so happily in love.

Alec's comings and goings since she arrived were becoming more and more a habit she loved. His joyful personality and tenderness were easy to be around. He knew just when she needed a soft touch and sympathetic ear and she enjoyed that closeness. Sometimes when she was alone she feared they were going too fast, but when they were together, everything was right.

Alec handled it all perfectly. He hadn't seemed overly upset when he left and was teasing her so maybe it bothered her more than him. It would take time to get over being bushwhacked by Larry and Marie, but seeing Alec in action with Larry only reinforced her feelings for him.

Chapter 12

True to his word, Alec got a barbecue together complete with 20 or 30 of his closest friends. Party day dawned sunny and hot, typical August weather in the Midwest. Maddy and her houseguests had talked over old times until the wee hours of the morning. They were bumping around getting coffee and orange juice flowing the next morning when Aunt Polly arrived. After introductions they soon were soon visiting with each other like long lost friends over her famous apple coffeecake.

Aunt Polly had the honor of being the first guest invited to Maddy's very first, official barbecue. Being included pleased her a lot, so much so she offered to bring the potato salad and various homemade goodies.

Settling into her favorite chair in the kitchen, Aunt Polly listened in astonishment about the previous day's visitors and the entire fiasco that followed.

"You mean, this Larry person showed up and tried to talk you into going back to Chicago? Not one to think fast on his feet, I'd say. You should have called me. I would have brought my Louieville slugger along and taken care of things for you."

"Well, our girl handled things pretty well, and having a lawman for a boyfriend as back-up, didn't hurt."

"I still feel badly," Buffy said. "We both knew how Marie is, and we should have called you when she started talking about coming, especially when Larry showed up. Believe it or not, I had misgivings but Skip here, wouldn't listen." She poked at him playfully and he sat up straight in protest.

"Hey, you women are supposed to know what you're doing. And Marie, well, she's extra hard to say 'no' to. You know that, Maddy. But I must say you really put your foot down with both her and Larry. And it's about time."

"I should have done it before, but nothing ever seemed worth fighting with her about until now. I hope I didn't hurt her. She's going to have her share of that if she stays with Larry."

Alec watched the clock for most of the day. He almost wished it wasn't so quiet, being inside doing paperwork made it seem even longer. Finally his shift was over, and he headed home for a quick shower and change of clothes then over to Maddy's and the barbecue. He worried that seeing her Chicago friends again, nice as they were, might somehow make her homesick for the big city. It wasn't fair to think that, especially after meeting Larry Preston and seeing how he treated Maddy, but he still worried.

When he pulled up in front of Maddy's house, they were all lolling on the wicker lawn furniture on the porch.

"Hey, man. Don't ever go shopping with these two. They wore me out." Skip groaned getting up to help Alec unload the barbecue grill.

Maddy and Buffy helped with the grocery sacks and took them into the kitchen. Alec gave Maddy a quick kiss in passing, which turned into several more.

"Thank you. I've waited all day to do that."

"I hate to discourage such a good kisser, but the company is arriving early." Maddy pointed to several cars that had pulled up outside.

"Let them wait." His kissed her again, and Maddy couldn't help but melt right into it, leaving them both a little breathless. Buffy blundered in just then with an empty glass.

"Oh, I'm sorry about that but there's some guys here, big guys, and they want to know where to put the keg."

"Be right there, Buffy," Alec started to pull away but Maddy yanked him back.

"Just a minute, you tease. You finally get me to wait for that darn truck of yours to turn in my driveway and then you leave me for a keg." She crossed her arms and looked away, waiting for his reaction.

"So you do wait at the window just to see me, huh? I thought so." He sounded pleased.

"I guess I do." Maddy's breath caught in her throat. "It kind of scares me. We've only been back together such a short time sometimes I think it's too good to be true. But then you leave and I can't wait for you to come back. I guess I worry you might not want to be stuck with me."

"Hey, don't worry about that. I know it's going fast, it is for me too. And I know that it worries you. But Maddy, don't think about it so much, it's like I've been waiting for you all my life. I don't want anything to ruin it either. It's a second chance for us."

"I was afraid when you heard what Larry said."

"Don't worry about Larry, that's in the past. You're my girl now. Just believe that."

"I believe." Maddy held his face in her hands, her heart beating with relief and joy. He said she was his girl, Maddy's heart beat even faster and she didn't hesitate to kiss him this time.

"We hate to break up a Kodak moment here, but there are people thirsting and starving outside this very door." Skip broke in with Buffy trying to pull him back.

"You big city people have lousy timing." Alec hugged Maddy and raised one eyebrow.

"No, just empty stomachs. What time is this shindig supposed to start? There are a lot of people here already. Come on." Skip yelled over his shoulder.

The old picnic table in the back was covered with a bright plastic tablecloth and Tim and some others set up a keg of beer with a washtub full of ice and pop.

Skip grabbed Alec and tied a big chef's apron on him. Maddy giggled when she read the bold, black letters on the front that said, "I love the chef." After cranking his head to read it, he frowned at Skip who in turn, pointed to Maddy.

"It's from her, man, not me."

"Thank goodness." Alec grimaced and caught Maddy's arm as she walked by. "Hey, do you? Love the chef, I mean?" Kissing him hard and quickly, Maddy just smiled and slipped away again without answering.

"Let's see how good you can cook before I commit myself." She grabbed a plate of raw hamburgers and gestured to the fast growing crowd.

The evening went fast, too fast. They ate, drank, played volleyball and Frisbee and cuddled by a fire later. But all too soon it was over and everyone began to leave with promises of getting together again. Her first house party was a success.

Buffy and Skip were up early for their return trip home.

"Okay, so here's the name and number of the landlord, just have him do the paperwork and send it to me to sign. Since I've got everything I need here, you can use whatever you want of my furniture. Just send the clothes and shoes and books. Well, here's a list. Just put everything else in storage. That way you'll be moved in before the wedding."

"Hey, deputy, how about a hand with the luggage? I'm creaking worse than an old door after all that volleyball last night." Skip winced, flexing achy arms while the girls said their goodbyes.

Following arm-in-arm, the girls hurried after them, giving each other instructions on a variety of things from the wedding to the apartment. For just a brief moment thoughts of going back to Chicago crossed Maddy's mind. It only took one look at Alec as he smiled and put his arm around her and the feeling passed.

The finality hit her; her old life was in the past, like her other childhood memories. Even though it was a little sad, the decision to stay was hers and she was content with it. Buffy poked her head out the window and madly waved goodbye as they drove down the street.

"Are you having second thoughts about staying now that they're leaving?"

Sighing, she shook her head. "No. Not really. Just going to miss my friends. Maybe it's the way my friendship with Marie ended. It was kind of a mixed up mess for a while, and I think I knew it would come to that. I've never been good at change. No, I'm not unhappy."

"A little sad is normal." He finished for her, and she nodded, leaning into his secure arms. "Well, Skippy and Buffy are great. I really like them. Not withstanding the fact that old Skip is a great volleyball player, the fact they picked you as a friend, shows good taste."

"Thanks for saying that. Meeting you again has changed my life, for the good I might add. I've been on my own for a long time, too long. Thank you for being patient."

"Sure, it shows my good taste, too." With that he tickled her and made a run for the house. "Come on, I've got to go to work at two, let's clean this place up. You know, I really hate leaving you, even to go to my job. It's beginning to interfere." Alec said with a mischievous look in her direction.

"Oh, come on. You know you'd never be happy if you weren't chasing the bad guys." She folded up some lawn chairs beside him.

"I like chasing you, too." His grin was irresistible. "Seriously, I like my job. But, maybe I don't like change any more than you do. I want it all and right now I feel like I'm almost there." He hugged her. "You know, you are a very pleasant distraction."

"You're changing the subject again. We were talking about your work. I'm beginning to see how dangerous it can be. But you're good at it and I trust you. I want you to be happy too. A relationship has to work for both of us."

"I think we're doing pretty well. And you're right. We both have to be happy. Are you happy?" He tugged at her chin and smiled.

"I sure am."

"Good. That's just what I wanted to hear. Okay. No use putting off going to work. Everything looks back to normal. I'll see you later. Get some rest and stop thinking so much." He touched the tip of her nose and she gave him an unhurried smile.

"Thanks for helping clean up and seeing Buffy and Skip off." Looking up at his tall frame, she felt like the luckiest girl in the world.

After Alec left, she gathered up the diary and letters and went out to the wicker lounger on the porch to read. The letters from Aunt Madeline's husband were so tender. They spoke of personal things, declarations of love and loyalty. Maddy felt a little guilty reading such private correspondence.

Wistfully she looked out over the quiet town, wondering how her Aunt had stood the loneliness for her husband over the years. She missed Alec the moment he left the room.

Maddy neatly refolded the letters and put them back in their envelopes. A yellow telegram fluttered to the floor. The wording was how Maddy had heard it in the movies. *We regret to inform you that your husband has been killed.* Maddy felt tears slide down her cheeks. It was dated June 6, 1944. Somewhere in France her husband had been killed. The words and warm sun lulled Maddy into a dreamy sleep of foreign beaches and war.

Some time later Alec woke her with a gentle kiss on the forehead. Smiling, she made room for him on the wicker lounger. "Hi. What time is it? I must have fallen asleep after you left."

She handed Alec a pillow and settled back with the diary. "I've read bits and pieces. The letters were sweet but nothing important. But wait until you hear what's in the diary. Maddy began to read softly.

Xmas Day 1924

What a strange way to spend Christmas, with the people at the diner. I love them like family. I heard my parents have stopped looking for me.

Alec shrugged, "So, they were looking for her then they quit."

"That was later. After she ran away she worked in a little diner on the East end of Chicago and seemed very happy away from the family."

"Funny, a kid with everything in those times and she runs away." Alec shook his head.

"You know what's really weird? Everyone was afraid of these people that I grew up hearing about, too. They were all intimidated. Now I know why, they were bullies and their children were bullies."

"Sounds like a dysfunctional family, no offense." Alec's blue eyes held a far-off stare as he settled snuggly beside her. "You think you know someone, trust them and then bam! Right between the eyes when you don't expect it."

"Sounds like you've had some bad experiences too." Maddy sat back pensively.

"What? Oh," he smiled sheepishly, "guess I got a little off the track, but, yeah, just forget it."

"These things have lain around all this time. A few more minutes won't hurt if you want to talk about it."

Alec sat silently for a minute and then took a deep breath. "I told you I was married briefly." Maddy nodded and looked into his face that was now hardened and distracted. "Well, I thought we were happy. But one day, she just up and left, filed for divorce and that was that. Didn't want to live in a small town, didn't want to be married to a man in law enforcement, not enough money. She had a long list of complaints. I guess she didn't want to be married. I just never thought I'd end up divorced. It really depressed me. About gave up on the notion of loving someone as much as I do now."

"Divorce isn't an end, at least not for us. It's given us this second chance." Maddy whispered.

"You don't mind? I thought maybe it was why you didn't want to talk about us, about getting serious." Alec's mood was somber, quiet.

"Alec, it's nobody's business what we've done before. You said that about Larry and me. I know you must have loved her very much to have married her. She's the loser, not you."

"I went on with my life, just wandering, my job and friends kept me sane. But when you came back to town, I started remembering things, feelings, about you and us, even when we were in junior high. Then I thought about a home, kids and all of it with you. It's why I probably pushed you sometimes. But in all fairness, we weren't total strangers."

"I suppose that is a true statement." She chuckled and settled back against his strong shoulder.

"The thought that maybe it was me that was holding you back, holding back what we could have, I just had to say something."

"I wasn't you at all. I appreciate you sharing that with

me." Maddy leaned over and kissed him. "Feel better?" He nodded and they went on reading the diary.

"Okay, now that we have that settled, it's back to my side of the family." She grinned and found her place.

"Okay, read on." Scanning the pages she sat bolt upright, her eyes wide.

"Alec, listen to this," she whispered breathlessly, "I think this might be what we were looking for."

May 16, 1925

Had terrifying meeting with two gangsters outside the diner tonight. They were going to kill the gangster Al Capone and I stumbled in on it. I pretended not to know what was going on, but told Capone to leave the diner by the back way. He did and no one got hurt.

Alec looked at Maddy and the diary with renewed interest.

June 1, 1925

Remember May 16? Today a man came to work and gave me money as a reward. I wouldn't take it because it was from Capone, for saving his life. I put him in his place and gave the dirty money back. No blood money for me.

June 20, 1925

Another man, more money. No!

July 10, 1925

Check arrived by mail, signed by Reginald J. Drake, a lawyer, but I know it's from Capone. Returned it immediately. Wish he'd leave me alone.

"Alec, my Aunt saved Al Capone's life, inadvertently, but he felt honor bound to repay the debt and she wouldn't accept it. I can hardly believe it."

"What's next? Go on." They hunched over the diary eagerly wanting to know more.

July 30, 1925

Capone is concerned that I won't take the money, but said I may be in danger from the killers. What have I done? He said he wanted to take care of me, but I said no again. He's a strange kind of man, said it was too bad he was married. Train ticket arrived in today's mail. I'm taking it.

Maddy scanned the next pages rapidly, outlining them for Alec. "She went to Omaha, later met Franklin and they were married. She's skipping months now. Here is the next one she wrote.

February 14, 1929

Newspaper article about killings in Chicago. Headline read St. Valentine's Day Massacre. They say gangster Al Capone ordered it. Seven men killed from another gang, how awful!

The next dozen faded pages were too faint to read, but when Maddy flipped to the end of the diary a newspaper clipping fell out.

Obituaries in the World: Alphonso Capone, also known as 'Scarface' Al Capone, died in Miami, at age 48. Born in Naples in 1899, died January 25, 1949, survivors include wife, Mae, one son Albert Francis "Sonny" his mother, three brothers and one sister. After years of illegal wealth, he died penniless.

"Incredible. Maddy, these documents might be worth a lot of money to a collector." Alec said, staring at them and then her. She leaned over into his arms, needing support.

"She should have let Al Capone take care of her rotten family." Maddy said bitterly. The anger in her voice surprised even her, Alec shook his head sympathetically.

"Maddy, she was strong enough to survive, just like we all are. Besides, if she'd let old Al Capone wipe out the family, where would that leave you?"

That thought had escaped her. She gave a little grin and then nodded in agreement. "I guess so, but she could have had him put a contract out on a couple of the more rotten ones."

"Why, you little gangster, you know you don't mean that. I know I'd be mighty disappointed if you hadn't been born, Maddy, mighty disappointed. So I should thank your family for that, for you." Rocking her like a small child, Alec felt her tears drop on his arm. How he wanted to comfort and protect her. How he loved her.

Maddy called Tommy the next day to help finish cleaning out the attic while she went to the store to make copies of the letters and diary. They were all going straight to a lock box in the bank as soon as she finished transcribing them.

The other was a heart stopper. The letter came from an attorney, the same attorney mentioned in her aunt's diary that had signed a check she returned. Reginald J. Drake. Maddy wondered if he was any relation to Jack Drake, Aunt Madeline's lawyer. Something she needed to check out later.

This could be very important. This was the actual proof of the missing bonds. She'd never heard of the company, but knew who to call back in Chicago who did.

The company had been sold several times and even gone through a name change to the Benton Mining Company. Now all she had to do was find the actual paper bonds. There was one little hitch, however. The bonds were called bearer bonds, meaning that whoever had them could redeem them for the cash value. According to the records they hadn't been cashed in yet, but anyone who found them could get the money. Since Maddy didn't know where they were, this could mean disaster. She could hardly wait to tell Alec.

She walked around the house, chilled, rubbing her arms and feeling uneasy. She heard Tommy making noise in the attic as he cleaned out the rest of the junk but even so she felt as if someone was lurking around, watching her. She hated that feeling. The weather hadn't helped either, rainy and windy and the one upstairs bedroom had leaked again. That would have to be fixed soon.

She went back into the library and started transcribing the diary by hand. This had to be what the mystery was all about, the bonds. Someone thought they were valuable, the question was now, where were they? If they did exist would they be worth anything? Her father's friend in Chicago said they were. Someone else thought so, too.

She needed to talk to Alec but he was still at work. Nervous, Maddy called his number but his secretary said he was out of the office, and no, he didn't answer his cell phone. Darn. It would have to keep. Suddenly she remembered Tommy again, she should go help him. Carefully she gathered up all her notes, the letters and diary and put them into plastic bags and tucked them safely out of sight in a canister in the kitchen.

Upstairs Tommy was sitting, resting among the old clothes, newspapers, and boxes. Maddy handed him a can of pop and he grinned, gratefully.

"Hey, thanks Miss Maddy, I sure am thirsty."

"Well, Tommy, you don't have to work yourself to death up here." She looked around in astonishment. "Goodness, I thought this would take a couple days and you're almost done."

"Aw, it wasn't so hard. Most of them boxes piled up in the corner were empty. I just smashed them flat." His face clouded, "Miss Maddy, I did accidentally knock a little hole in the wall when I was in that bedroom though. I'm awful sorry, the doorstopper is gone and the knob went through because of the rain and, I can fix it though. I helped Miss Madeline once before in the same spot, we put wads of paper and she made glue out of flour. It was fun."

Jumping up excitedly he wanted to fix it then and there, but Maddy sat back and shook her head. "Tommy, don't worry about it. You come back tomorrow and we'll fix it properly with some plaster. Come on downstairs and I'll pay you for today."

They chatted amiably as they went downstairs carrying armloads of garbage sacks, it was getting late by the time they said good-bye. A half hour later, hamburgers sizzled on the stove and a salad was tossed and waiting for Alec while she sat daydreaming.

"I thought I told you to keep the doors locked." Alec stood in the doorway, hands on hips, a disapproving look on his face. Maddy jerked back to the present.

"Oh, I guess I forgot to lock it when Tommy left a little while ago, sorry."

"You've got to be more careful." Shaking his head, he took off his gun belt and hat and laid them on the counter. Taking her in his arms, he chuckled, "I sure can't stay mad at you for very long. Like maybe thirty seconds. What were you thinking so hard about?"

"Well, to make a long story short, Al Capone invested money, the money my aunt wouldn't accept, in the stock market. Even though it crashed in 1929, she didn't lose it all. In this last letter, his attorney is supposed to have sent the actual bonds to her. Get this: $20,000.00 worth and that was back then." Eager to hear more, Alec's dark eyes widened and he gave a low whistle as he settled into a kitchen chair.

"So, where are they?"

"I said I found out what we were looking for, not where they are. I just hope she didn't toss them like Leland thinks she did."

"Hmmm, twenty thousand dollars in 1929 was a lot of money then. If the company's still solvent it could be worth a lot."

"It is. I called a friend of my dad's on the stock exchange, it changed names, sold or something, and it's still worth a lot of money if you have the actual bonds."

"Wow, again. Maddy this could mean a lot to you, moneywise."

"I'm not going get my hopes up, yet. But A.C. is definitely Al Capone, everything fits, names, dates and places. And because she wouldn't accept the money, he hired someone to make the investments for her. Look, I copied them." Handing the copies with her notes on them to Alec, he began to read intently.

"There are seven or eight letters. The first one is okay, but the rest are only partly readable. The third and fourth ones indicate the investment being done for her without her knowledge and then this one, this is cool," she pulled up a chair close to his and flipped the pages, "the very last letter is typed, written by his attorney. This says it all."

"Okay, I see. He sent her the bonds and said to keep everything to her self."

Maddy sat back smugly, passing the hamburgers. "I rest my case. She was left a legacy by old Al Capone himself, for saving his life. Isn't this awesome?"

"Sure sounds that way." Alec leaned back in the chair thinking hard. "But where are they? Did she accept them? Give them away, or burn them?"

"Well, that's the question we all want answered." Maddy said putting the papers down neatly, her story loosing momentum. "That's all I found out."

"Well, that's a lot more than we knew before. I've been thinking about that all afternoon, too. What would she have done with a bunch of paper bonds? There has to be another safe deposit box or a secret hiding place." Alec folded his arms thoughtfully.

"Where would someone keep bonds?" Alec wondered aloud.

Just then the doorbell rang and they both looked guiltily at each other. "Let's not say anything to anyone yet." She said quickly and Alec agreed.

"Hey, Leland, what brings you out and about? You look a little rushed." Alec said as Maddy returned with Leland Lancaster following. Nodding a greeting to Alec, he sat down and accepted a cup of coffee

"I've been busy, real busy, is how I've been. I came across a few things that don't add up concerning your aunt's estate, Maddy."

"Like what?" Alec and Maddy exchanged uneasy glances.

"I want you to know I just found these copies stuck together in a file among her income tax records. They were in some things Jack Drake brought down from Omaha. I don't know if he meant to give them to me, they were folded and stuck to some other folders. They date back to God knows when, 1925, I think, when Drake's grandfather ran the firm. Anyway, they indicated she owned over twenty thousand dollars in corporate bearer bonds. She filed this in 1952, acknowledged the interest in subsequent tax years and then all of a sudden, the year she took ill, they disappear from her records." Leland looked upset and frustrated. "I just hope the taxes and such have been kept up."

"These bearer bonds, are they good?" Maddy sat forward expectantly.

"Good? Good is a mild word for it. I wish I owned five hundred dollars worth. If they were bought in 1929, they bought cheap because of the crash. Those bearer bonds have multiplied in value by now. They could be worth a small fortune!"

Alec whistled and looked at Maddy, her father's friend was right. The bonds were still worth something.

"Well, I'm no mathematician, but I can tell you twenty thousand dollars worth of bonds will be six or seven figures today. But what's bad is--"

"What could possibly be bad about six or seven figures or more, Leland?" Maddy said excitedly, her voice high pitched at the thought of no more money worries.

"Let me finish. The bad thing is bearer means just that. Whoever has them can convert them into cash or transferred into common stock. And that means whoever has them can cash them."

The three of them exchanged looks. Alec placed a hand on Maddy's arm.

"So, someone else knows about this then?" Maddy said and sat down, her bubble popped in front of her.

"I don't know. But I used to think she destroyed them, and she might have but look around. She didn't spend anything frivolous on herself. Probably didn't know their worth, especially after they sold or resold the company. Then, she forgot all about them. We just don't know what she did with them. This is very unsettling."

"It might just be an old treasure story, you know, the old widow with wealth hidden under the mattress, especially since she didn't want the money, she might have gotten rid of it." Leland injected and then sighed and waved his hands.

"I lived about here all my life and I never heard any rumors like that, and I heard them all." Alec said and looked at Maddy.

"Well, I have to get home, I'm beat." Leland got up to go, "I'm going to call Jack Drake, her attorney in Omaha, tomorrow. Maybe he knows something. It's probably before his time, he didn't take over the practice until the late 60s, but maybe there are more records."

"Leland, I do appreciate your trying." Maddy extended her hand and he grasped it, smiling.

"It's my pleasure. It's the least I could do for Nielsen's newest citizen. Do be careful until this thing is straightened out. Someone might believe any story having to do with easy money."

Shutting the door behind him, Maddy looked at Alec, even more puzzled than before.

"One minute I'm sure he's in on it and the next one he's trying to help." Alec threw up his hands. "Maybe you're right Maddy and he's just an astute businessman."

"Do you think we should tell him about the Al Capone connection?" She asked tentatively.

"I don't trust him that much yet." Alec replied grimly, but shrugged, "I don't know. Let's wait a little while longer."

"Come on, we've got work to do." Maddy pulled him along.

"Work? What work? What I have in mind wouldn't be considered work, my Love." Pushing and prodding, Maddy made her way to the library and stood in front of a solid paneled wall. Patting the old wood, she smiled at him. "This is it. Start going over every inch of this paneling and see if there's a hidden compartment. It's the only thing we haven't tried." Alec rolled his eyes.

"Maddy, you watch entirely too much TV." But dutifully he started tapping on the polished wood surfaces.

Chapter 13

Maddy awoke the next morning with sore knuckles and the knowledge that Alec had wanted to do more than knock on wood last night. A good jog in the country would help clear her brain as she tried to figure out where they could look for her aunt's missing bonds.

It was already warm for early morning, so she put on shorts and a tee shirt, cinching up her worn running shoes she stretched and got ready to run. Good thing she was running early; later it was going to be really hot. She headed for her favorite trail, the one with softly rolling hills and little farmsteads tucked here and there.

Maddy was so intent on her thoughts she only casually noticed the sound of an engine behind her. She moved closer to the edge and kept up her pace. Only after it passed did she feel apprehensive. Two men in a beat-up old pick-up whistled and shouted, speeding by and leaving her in a cloud of dust. What a mean trick. Closing her eyes against the grit that settled around her, she suddenly saw the brake lights go on and the vehicle back up.

In her haste to get going this morning, she'd forgotten her mace can. The man hanging out the passenger window kept yelling and Maddy whirled and went the opposite way. They turned around and pulled alongside and leered at her.

"Hey, Baby, need a lift? I could go for a girl like you." Vile laughter and comments soon grew more and more suggestive until she panicked and changed direction again. They quickly followed and her stomach rolled with fear, she knew she was in trouble.

Pulling their rattletrap vehicle in front, they expertly blocked her way. Quickly she turned and went the other direction once more but they were too quick for her and blocked any escape route. Bending over to catch her breath, she glared at them and tried to think.

"If you're thinking of screaming, scream all you want, Missy. There's no one to hear you way out here." He laughed and grabbed her arm. Maddy kicked him as hard as she could. The useless gesture just made him angrier and his grip tightened.

"Hey, save some for me. I don't like them bruised." The other man was getting out of the truck when a tremendous explosion ripped through the air. Maddy stopped struggling and looked up to see a tractor racing over the hill with one of her friendly farmers she always waved at hunched over the wheel. She'd never seen a tractor move so fast, and then she realized he was holding a shotgun in one hand and charging like John Wayne to the rescue.

The cowboy hesitated a minute and loosened his grip

enough that she could jerk away, running towards the green John Deere tractor. Angrily they cursed and climbed back into their old truck, gunning the engine and making gravel fly behind them in their haste to escape. Maddy had never been so glad to see anyone in her life.

"You okay, there Miss? Darn bums come around stealing gas and fertilizer or digging up the ditches for wild marijuana. Dang dopers. You catch your breath and I'll take you into town." Propping the very large gun on the even bigger tractor tire, he took off a battered straw hat, wiping the band with his handkerchief. His tan face looked like wrinkled leather but held crisp blue eyes and a square jawed, jaunty grin.

"Never seen the like, every year it gets worse." He muttered again then helped her up on the tractor. "You're Miss Madeline's kin, I hear. Been seeing that young deputy, too. I'm the one who farms that eighty acres across the road. I wave at you when you run by. You're mighty quick, too." Speechless, Maddy nodded. "By the way, I'm Ezra Mick."

"I'm pleased to meet you, Mr. Mick. And thanks for the rescue, but how do you know so much about me?"

"Small town, miss, everyone knows everything about everybody." Ezra revved up the engine and with her carefully perched on the fender, they headed off down the road, a spotted dog trotting happily alongside. A long drive way led to a rambling farmhouse surrounded by neat, red farm out buildings. An elderly woman stood on the porch, cats scattered all around her feet.

"Howdy, missus, everything's all right now. I just ran off a couple of bums trying to scare off our little jogger, here. Shep and I scared the pants off of them, didn't we boy?"

The old man cackled and lit a pipe while the dog barked in agreement.

"Are you okay, my dear?" The older woman looked from one to the other with concern. Maddy assured her she was fine. "I worry more about you and that darn gun, Old Man. You're too old to go around the countryside shooting it up. This isn't Dodge City." She chided him lovingly, but he just patted her arm and they headed for town and a talk with the deputy.

After talking to Alec privately, the old farmer named Ezra tipped his hat and left. Alec led Maddy to his office and shut the door with a bang. The old venetian blinds swung wildly in the wake of his anger.

"Maddy, what in the world were you thinking of? Obviously, you weren't thinking. Going jogging by yourself after all that's been going on. You could have been hurt, or worse."

Maddy squirmed on the cold, hard chair and fumed inwardly. Of course he was right; that's what made it so hard to listen to.

"Oh, Alex, I don't think..."

"That's right! You hit the nail on the head. You didn't think!" Throwing a file on the desk, he sat down in his squeaky chair running a hand through his hair in frustration. Pointing a finger at her he was about to continue when she finally had enough.

"I understand I shouldn't have gone that way and gone alone, but I forgot. I was so wrapped up in thinking about the diary. Besides, I don't think those two guys were involved, just a couple of flirts, out for good time. Don't you think?" Alec didn't looked like he was convinced and she sat back, chewing on her fingernail. "You were busy and couldn't jog this morning," she finished weakly. "One of them did look familiar. I just can't recall from where."

Alec drew his lips in thoughtfully. "Are you sure?"

She nodded miserably. "I'm not sure where, though."

"I'll tell you one thing. Good old boys around here don't need two blasts from a shotgun to get their attention Maddy. Old Ezra said he'd never seen them before, that means they're outsiders and could be drug dealers and dangerous."

Alec came around the desk and knelt in front of her quickly, "Ezra said one had his hands on you. He didn't hurt you or anything, did he?" His thumb rubbed against her skin and gave her goose bumps. She shook her head and burrowed in his arms, loving the concern in his voice.

So full of rage only a moment ago, his voice now softened to a tender whisper and he touched her arms smudged with grime where she'd been grabbed.

Tears welled up in her eyes at his obvious concern and she cupped his face in her hands. The emotion in that one look they exchanged tore at her heart.

"No, darling deputy, they didn't hurt me, honest. Scared me pretty good, but that's all. I'm really sorry I acted so foolishly and made you worry. I won't do it again, I promise."

"Thank goodness Ezra was there. He's had a lot of trouble with drug dealers and thefts lately. If anything ever happened to you I don't know what I'd do." Pulling Maddy up from the chair into his arms, Alec kissed her hard, burying his face in her copper hair. A tap on the door and Alec's secretary interrupted them with business. Reluctantly they parted.

"Sorry, Alec, State Patrol is on line one."

"Okay, thanks Brenda. Maddy, I'm having Ben drive you home. No argument." Alec kept holding her hand.

"No argument there, Alec." She sidled up to him and leaned her head on his shoulder for a moment before easing out of the office. "I am sorry."

Ben, the tall officer who'd helped investigate the break-in at her house waited to drive her. She sighed and just wished she were at home. He smiled when he saw her come out of Alec's office, and reached for his hat.

"Come on. Alec said no stops along the way."

"Oh, don't worry about that. I just want to go home."

"Miss Morris, Alec said to remind you to lock up after I leave." Ben had dutifully gone around the house and checked the doors and windows and everything was in its proper place.

"Thanks, Ben. Tell Alec to call me when he gets off."

"I think he'll be over, if I know him." Ben said with a knowing smile. The house seemed emptier than usual. Maddy had so much company lately it was hard to get used to the silence. Relaxing in a hot bath, she felt better after dressing in fresh clothes. Thinking she heard someone at the back door, she padded down the hallway hoping Alec got off early to be with her. Being physically threatened had given her a little more perspective on needing someone. It felt good to have Alec in her life.

The clock chimed loudly from the living room and Maddy felt strange, in fact, everything around her had a strange feel to it. Just as she reached the end of the hall a hand came out of the closet and dirty fingers clasped over her mouth and cheeks.

Automatically Maddy pulled back and struggled, there

was something familiar about the smell. An arm encircled her waist and pulled her back into the darkness of the closet. *Oh no! The sweat and beer smell. That cowboy this morning had the same smell. How? How could he have gotten in? Ben and she both checked everything.* That was of little consequence now. A criminal stood here in her home and controlled her.

Think, girl, think! Try and talk to him, see what he wants. But she couldn't, he wouldn't let her. His filthy hand pressed onto her mouth and chin so hard she couldn't breathe, much less talk. *Stay calm and you'll stay alive. Maddy, don't panic, think of Alec.* She did and it helped.

"You listen and you listen good. I want all the papers, those letters and the book, the diary. I know you have them and I want them *now.* " The dirty cowboy jerked her hard and moved his hand slightly so she could reply.

"What letters and book?" She gasped. But her try at stalling only angered him. Viciously he jerked her arms and pulled her head back by the hair, his mouth next to her ear.

"Don't make me mad, Girl. You made me mad this morning. Now where are they?"

"In the kitchen," she croaked. He pushed her forward again giving her no time to think. Maddy pointed to the refrigerator and stepped back but he kept his hands on her.

Flinging the freezer door open, he found the plastic bag with the papers and diary in them. With a gleeful curse he grabbed the frosty bag and pulled her back down the hall towards the front door. Terrified, she knew he might hurt or even kill her now that he had what he wanted.

The hall rug balled up under their feet as he dragged her forward. The little table with the porcelain bird crashed behind them. One arm slipped loose and she flailed out, hoping to touch anything stable but he was too strong for her.

He pressed her up against the door as he peered through the sheer curtains, muttering under his breath looking for his partner. She nearly slipped away but he roughly slapped her across the face, leaving her dazed.

At that moment, her free hand found the umbrella stand and the big silk umbrella with a duck's head handle. Her groping fingers closed over it and she swung it around, hard, smacking him on his neck and back. Harder and harder she hit, as fast as she could. Suddenly her other arm was free and she regained her balance.

Using her feet she kicked and bashed away at the intruder until she realized he was backing away from her. In his haste he broke a pane of glass opening the front door trying to get away. He swung the door open just as Maddy bent forward and charged into it, hitting her soundly in the forehead. She sank down and in a cascade of stars. She screamed as she felt herself being lifted and slammed into something very hard. There was just blissful silence as she collapsed on the floor.

When she opened her eyes again, faces peered down at her in a circle. They looked familiar but pulsated in and out like some bad dream. It scared her and she tried to get away, but hands pushed her back down. Even if she had managed to get up, the pain in her head would have forced her right back down.

Alec's voice gently called her name from somewhere in the distance and then his steel blue eyes and crooked grin came into focus. She smiled and put a hand out. Groggy and shaky she tried to speak, but he kissed her gently and made the other 'faces' go away.

Alec was here, he wouldn't let anyone hurt her. Maddy could go to sleep. She was safe with Alec. A moment later a light shining in her eyes made her turn away, groaning in protest. The sharp pain from the movement aggravated her headache even more. Why didn't they leave her alone? She just wanted to sleep. She raised one arm to shield her eyes but someone pulled it back down and poked her arm. A wire or IV seemed to be attached to it.

Prying her lids open Maddy licked dry lips and saw another circle of faces. Not so many this time, and not directly above her. It took a moment to get it all in focus. Everything was white. White walls, sheets, the nurses and the doctor in front of her. There were tubes in her arm and someone said, "She's coming out of it."

"What's the other guy look like?" she quipped painfully.

"Well, I heard you broke an umbrella over his head, so probably worse. But he gave you a couple of good whacks with something hard before you went down, Miss Morris. Anything else hurt?"

The doctor looked at her intently, he was young and nice looking and very professional. Maddy shifted around, not sure what hurt and what didn't until a pain in her shoulder made her gasp.

"Ouch! Shoulder, hurts. Shoulder definitely hurts." It was hard for Maddy to talk.

"Yes, it was nearly dislocated, but with rest it will be fine. Now that you're awake and seem to be focusing, I'd say you're going to be fine in no time. Slight concussion, sprained shoulder and lots of bumps and bruises, but we'll keep you overnight for observation. By the way, I'm Dr. Richards. If you need anything push the buzzer."

Maddy's lips were dry and she felt like she was in a fog.

"You others can stay a few minutes, but let her rest. She can probably go home in a day or two." Maddy heard Alec and the doctor talking quietly in the shadows and then the door close.

"Hey, how's my girl?" Alec leaned over and kissed her sweetly on the cheek, concern welling in his eyes.

"Alec, how did he get in? Ben and I both checked everything."

Tears of anger and pain filled her eyes, and she tried to rise up on her elbow as the memory flooded back.

"He broke in after you got home, Honey, we found a screen and broken window in the basement. It wasn't your fault, if anyone's it was mine. I should have known they'd try again." Alec dropped his hat and tried to calm her. An efficient looking nurse came in when she heard the commotion and frowned.

"Miss Morris, this will never do. You're not to upset yourself or I'll have to give you a sedative." She looked sternly at both of them, and they nodded.

Clutching Alec's hand, Maddy slid back down on the pillows and closed her eyes, her head throbbing.

"Alec, it was the same man who stopped me on the road, the dirty cowboy. He was waiting. He grabbed me. I tried to fight."

"Maddy, you did just fine. Try not to think about it anymore. It'll be okay. We'll talk tomorrow, just get some rest now. I'll be right here." Tucking the sheet around her, he settled in a chair beside the bed. Worriedly he kissed her hand that clutched his. "I'll be right here," he repeated softly and with a sigh she fell asleep.

* * *

"Alec, I'm perfectly capable of walking on my own two feet." Maddy protested as she leaned over and opened the front door of her house after being released from the hospital. "Honestly. I got a bump on my head, not my feet. Won't you put me down?" Alec's grip only tightened.

"No. Your doctor kept you an extra day because of the headaches. He said rest and no strain whatsoever."

"And between the two of us," Aunt Polly continued, sweeping down the hall from the kitchen, a dish rag in her hand, "We're going to make sure you follow orders. When Alec isn't here, I will be." She hefted her Louisville Slugger baseball bat to her shoulder, "This time I'm going to be prepared."

Maddy looked from one to the other, her heart full of love for them and their concern. "Well, it looks like there's no room for discussion then. Carry on."

Aunt Polly led the way into the bedroom where Alec carefully laid Maddy on the freshly made bed. The pillows were plumped up, the sun streamed in the windows and the room looked so inviting. She was home.

Gently Alec sat on the edge of her bed and gave her a little kiss. A large bandage covered the bump on her head and she winced at the slight jostling.

"I'm sorry, did I hurt you?"

Maddy shook her head which was a mistake and meekly answered, "No, I did."

"I'm going to make sure no one ever hurts you again, Maddy. You've got my word." Alec promised. "You know, when I saw you lying on the floor, I thought you were dead.

My heart almost stopped beating. I'm going to find this guy, Maddy and when I do..."

"...You'll arrest him and be the professional that you are, deputy. Whether it's for me or for someone else. I'll be proud that you did it that way, Alec. Your love has given me something to hold on to. Something I've never had before. I don't want to lose it."

"I couldn't agree more. So you did a lot of thinking while you were recuperating?" His thumb stroked the hand he held in a simple gesture and with a slow, secret smile she nodded.

Chapter 14

Maddy didn't get to go to Buffy and Skip's wedding because she hadn't fully recovered from the results of her attack. So, she and Alec sent a wonderfully lavish present, crystal stemware they ordered online and had it delivered to try to make up for it.

Visits from friends helped while away the hours. Tommy stopped by regularly, and every visit he brought her something, a book of poetry, flowers and card games. Bubba and the others stopped by too, and with Alec they'd watch video's or played cards.

One afternoon Alec saw a strange car in the driveway and hurried inside. Maddy and Dr. Richards were enjoying a good laugh and when he walked in they seemed to sober up quickly. The doctor didn't leave for over an hour, and afterwards Alec actually acted a little jealous of the doctor's close attention to his patient.

"What did he want?" Alec finally asked, "I mean the hospital released you. I didn't know doctors made house calls anymore, and out-of-town house calls at that?"

"He was on his way home from a seminar and he just stopped by to see how I was." Maddy explained in amusement.

"You realize I hardly get any alone time with you anymore. I admit it, I'm envious."

"Oh, come on, jealous of a teenager who keeps me from being bored to tears when you're not here, and now, the poor, devoted doctor who healed me. Actually I think Aunt Polly called him, she's worried about my headaches." Alec looked relieved.

"Well, that's different. Between your recovery and my running all over on this case, we haven't had much time alone together lately, and I miss it. Guess I'm being silly, huh?" He sat down on the bed beside her, looking contrite. "How are the headaches?"

"They're better, really. Dr. Richard said they'll be less and less. So, I'm fine." She leaned over and kissed him. "But thanks for worrying. By the way, do you know I simply adore a man in a uniform?"

"Great. That means I have to worry about every soldier, sailor or patrolman that stops you."

"Nope, only a cocky, deputy sheriff, and one I know in particular." Putting her arms around his neck, she drew him close. The curve of his shoulder fit her head comfortably.

"I sure wish I didn't have to go on this stupid trip tomorrow." He tucked the sheets around her, looking concerned.

"I'll be fine. The doctor said I'll finally be able to get out of bed now. Besides, Aunt Polly will be here. Just go so you can get back."

"Oh, I'll be back, it's not an overnight trip so you can count on that, just a long day. I know you're disappointed about losing the letters and diary and things. We might still find them."

"I doubt it. At least I have the copies I made, but you know one thing I really wish? That we could have found those stocks, it sure would have made life better for the whole town."

"What do you mean?" Alec held her carefully.

"Well, I'd like to fix this place up for a bed and breakfast. It's huge, the whole upstairs is bedrooms, but we'd need to add on more bathrooms and, well, I have a lot of other ideas. What do you think? Isn't that a good idea?"

"It's a great idea."

"We wouldn't have had to worry about money if we could have found Aunt Madeline's bonds. I was even thinking if they had been worth as much as Leland thought, it would have been enough to start a small library in town. But, it's only wishful thinking now. Someone's got those bonds and they're just waiting to cash them in. That's what makes me so mad."

"That's awfully generous of you, Maddy, but then, it's one more reason I love you so much."

"Well, thank you for that. I can be generous with pretend money. But, it's only a pipe dream now. No money. No library, maybe no bed and breakfast inn if I don't get things figured out."

"Just don't worry so much, I said I'd help you. Promise me, or I won't leave." Her kiss reassured him.

While he was gone, Maddy had a lot of time to think and plan. The constant worry of having no money faded with the generosity of her aunt. To make it last, she had to manage her money sensibly. An earnest search for solvency grew and the bed and breakfast seemed the best idea.

A call to the local printer gave her some ideas on advertising. But she'd have to go over the status of the house with Alec next. It might not even be possible if the house wasn't in good shape.

"Maddy, your idea has sure got folks in town excited." Aunt Polly exclaimed as she sat down next to her in the kitchen the next day.

"Well, it's all in the planning stages yet so it's not a done deal. But Alec agrees it's a perfect answer to the problem of keeping a big house going." Maddy agreed excitedly. "There's so much that needs to be done yet. Alec said it might be a workable plan. He's got someone to check the water pipes and the wiring later next week. His friend Bubba already fixed that leak in the roof so Tommy and I can get at that damaged wall in the extra bedroom. We can at least do that. Tommy's coming over tomorrow, in fact."

"You sure you feel up to working like this?"

"Oh yes, Aunt Polly, I'm feeling fine. I haven't had any headaches now for a while. It's time I started doing a few things. I think I'll putter around outside, it's so nice out."

Later Aunt Polly found her weeding the corner flower garden when she brought her a glass of lemonade.

"Isn't it a little hot for you to be doing this?" There was disapproval in her voice.

"Oh, it's just so good to get out of the house. I'm taking it easy but that drink looks wonderful. Thank you. This is just what I needed." Maddy took off her gardening gloves and touched her forehead with the icy glass before taking a sip.

"I thought you said you weren't going to overdo it." Aunt Polly nodded towards the pile of weeds stacked beside her.

"That is a lot of weeds, isn't it?" Maddy looked a little sheepish. "But I was enjoying myself and I didn't realize how much time had gone by." She shrugged and sat on her knees.

"Well, I do. Too much time to be in this hot sun." Alec's voice boomed from the driveway.

"Alec, you're back. Welcome home." Maddy stood up and was greeted affectionately by Alec. "Wow, you are a sight for sore eyes. Hey, what are you doing?" Maddy said with a surprised laugh as he swept her up into his arms, heading towards the front porch.

"You are not supposed to be working so hard." He said in a firm but kind tone and deposited her in the wicker lounge chair.

Maddy was about to argue but when Aunt Polly came up behind him with her arms crossed, she sat back meekly.

"I guess I did enough today anyway, I can't fight you both. But, Alec, I've had some more ideas about the house, let me tell you about it."

"Okay, but I've got some news that will interest you too. Who goes first?" He sat in a chair next to her.

"You go first. The look on your face tells me it's important. Is it something we've been waiting to hear about the guy who attacked me?"

"Aunt Polly, there's news." She called out to her friend.

"What news? What's going on, Alec?" Hurriedly Aunt Polly sat down.

"I just checked in at the office and thought you'd like to know they found that van matching the description of the one outside the house, only thing was there was a body in it."

"A body?" Maddy sat forward, horrified, her hand covering her mouth. "Who was it? Anyone we know?"

"From the description, I'd say it was your dirty cowboy. A white male, about twenty-five, long, dark hair, cowboy shirt with torn sleeves. His name was Fred Simmons and he has a record."

"How awful, Alec. I won't have to identify him or anything, will I?" Maddy shuddered.

"No, he's already been identified. I'll take care of it. I saw him as well as you did that day. Don't worry."

"'Don't worry, he says'. A man who attacks Maddy is dead. Who killed him?" Aunt Polly snorted and leaned forward.

"That's awful. As bad as what he did to me, I'd never wish him dead." The thought made her shiver just thinking about it. She still had nightmares about being attacked in her own home. "I just want all that stuff behind us and not have to think about it any more. I think I understand now why my aunt didn't want to have anything to do with a gangster and that money. It's brought nothing but grief."

Alec thought for a moment then swiftly dropped to one knee, holding her hand tightly.

"I wasn't going to do this now, but maybe now is the time. Maddy, I love you and I'm asking you to marry me. I don't care if you want a long engagement, but I just have to ask now or bust wide open."

In shocked silence, Maddy covered his hand with hers; she was overcome and didn't hesitate for a moment. She could only nod. A million happy thoughts were racing through her mind. Slowly she pulled him up, kissed his strong hands and whispered, "Yes."

Fumbling in his pocket, with shaking hands he produced a jeweler's box and slowly opened it. A lovely diamond engagement ring sparkled from the black velvet nest. Trembling, she held out her hand and he slipped the ring on her finger. Tears slid down Maddy's cheeks. But they were tears of joy.

"We're going to have a wonderful life, Maddy. With lots of kids. No looking back."

"And a hunting dog for you." They both laughed and held onto each other tightly, "What a deal." She said happily.

Maddy and Alec joyfully prepared for their wedding. After much discussion they decided to go for the bed and breakfast plan. They wanted to wait until they got it going first, but Aunt Polly decided to make plans for both the wedding and the inn and blatantly took responsibility for them.

The whole town of Nielsen seemed caught up in the young couple's life, and Maddy couldn't have been happier to share their joy with the town. Things never seemed so good. In honor of her aunt, Maddy decided to wear Aunt Madeline's wedding gown she had found carefully saved in one of the trunks. The satin dress had turned a soft golden color from being in storage. The simple line suited Maddy and would be her 'something old' and 'something borrowed'.

Preparing the rooms for the guests took a lot more work. The one bedroom with water damage on the wall needed to be fixed immediately, the wallpaper hung in tatters. With Tommy's help it was the last room to need major repair.

"Well Tommy, this is the last and worst of it. When we're done, we'll tackle the fence and garden outside. Isn't this a mess?" Maddy curled up her nose at the mustiness.

"No sweat, Miss Maddy." Tommy's happy-go-lucky attitude brightened up the nasty chore.

"Yeah, Miss Madeline and I fixed this very wall a long time ago. I was just a little kid then." Maddy smiled to herself at his description. "She didn't have anything to stuff in the hole so we went up to the attic and got a bunch of papers she said weren't any good for nothing anymore, and stuffed them in there. Then she used paste and covered it with wallpaper, and it was good as new. She paid me for that too."

Maddy, working hard, only half-listened to his story. The old fashioned glue was brittle and lumpy and fell in dry clumps, making the clean up a little easier.

"Aunt Madeline certainly stuffed enough of this paper in there, didn't she?" Maddy commented to Tommy as they worked.

"Yeah, she sure did get mad when the roof leaked, said she'd fix this hole good and proper." Tommy chuckled at his memory.

About the same time Maddy noticed the printing on the papers, the words Tommy spoke caught her attention. "'We got these papers from the attic she said weren't worth nothing.'" Jerking her head up, she looked at Tommy seriously, her heart pounding.

"What did you say, Tommy? About the papers you used?"

"What about the papers?"

"About the papers you stuffed in the wall. You said you and Miss Madeline got them from the attic. What kind of papers were they? What did they say on them? Do you recall?"

He shrugged again and kept on working.

"Tommy, this is really important. Very important. Please try and remember, you said Aunt Madeline said they weren't worth anything?" Tommy thought a moment and then nodded. Maddy looked from the crumbling wall to Tommy and back again.

"Yeah, they looked like giant money, paper money. But she just stuffed them inside the wall and plugged the hole and pasted them all over to make it smooth for the wallpaper. It looked real neat, too."

Maddy sat back on her heels, staring at the wall and grinning. The corner of a piece of paper caught her eye. Carefully she pulled the old wallpaper away, the glue cracked and dropped at her feet. Finally a large piece pulled away to reveal an entire section of wall neatly papered with the missing bonds!

"See, that's what I told you. Yep, that's them all right, the old papers. Gee, they look pretty good yet, don't they?"

"Yes, Tommy." She hugged him tightly, "They look real good. You are a genius. We found them. We found the missing bonds, Tommy. They were here all the time, and we didn't even realize it."

She jumped up and down and hugged him again, and doing a little jig in the midst of the mess.

Tommy looked at her as if she'd lost her mind.

"I've got to tell Alec and Aunt Polly. Now Tommy, this is very important. Don't touch the wall. Don't do any more work on the wall until we show Aunt Polly and Alec, okay?"

He squinted up at the wall and shrugged, nodding. "Gee, if they were worth something, I sure wouldn't have used them."

"It wasn't your fault, Tommy. They probably weren't worth much when you used them. But they are now and I'm going to buy you something really special. Just don't go anywhere until I get back with Alec, okay?"

Maddy flew downstairs, nearing falling headlong on the rug in front of the front door as she grabbed the phone to call Alec. No answer. She ran to the back door and over to Aunt Polly's where Alec and she were calmly having a conversation by the back gate. When he saw her, he held fast food sacks up like a trophy.

"Alec! Come, quickly!" Maddy caught her breath and screamed his name. The look on her face and the urgency in her voice made him drop the food and start running, his hand on his pistol. Maddy could hardly speak, she was so excited. Aunt Polly came huffing and puffing behind him.

"Maddy, what's wrong? Is someone in the house?" She shook her head and took a deep breath before grabbing his hand and motioning them to follow her.

"No, nothing like that. It's not who's in the house, it's what's in the house. Oh, Alec, I've found them, or rather, Tommy and I found them. He's guarding them now, come on." Still shaking and half-crying in excitement Maddy started up the stairs with her friends close behind, still not sure what was wrong.

"What? Maddy, what did you find? Why is Tommy guarding anything?" Alec tried to calm her down.

"Okay, I'm sorry, I'm just so excited. But Alec, we found the missing bonds."

"You found them where?" Incredulous, he looked at Aunt Polly and then back at her.

"You've got to see this to believe it. They couldn't have been any safer than if they'd been in the bank. Come on." Pulling Alec along, they burst into the back bedroom where Tommy sat staring at the wall. Slowly Alec walked up to the section of torn wallpaper and looked at the neatly pasted bonds on the wall. He gazed closely at them and let out a whoop.

"Maddy, you hit the jackpot. I can't believe it."

Aunt Polly inched closer and removed her glasses as she clucked and shook her head in disbelief.

"That's a lot of money pasted on a wall. What are you going to do with it?" Alec looked at her.

"Not what am I going to do with it, you're going to be my husband, it's what are we going to do with it? Besides, I told you my dream. If what I think is true, the town of Nielsen just got a library and we got a bed and breakfast."

"Maddy, that's great. You still want to do that? You have the most generous heart. That way people won't think I married you just for your money. You're too good to be true and I love you." He was laughing and hugging Maddy. Aunt Polly and Tommy laughed and danced a little jig behind them.

"I was the richest woman in town before I found the money, Alec." Maddy stopped moving and looked up. Her smile was eager and alive with affection and pure delight as she hugged him tightly.

There was a steady stream of visitors to the house until professional wallpaper people came and carefully removed every scrap of the bonds from the wall. The newspaper did a big story on it, the news wires too. They totaled up everything, and Leland and the bank figured Maddy's bonds were worth several million dollars. Which Maddy promptly converted and sold to start the "Madeline O'Keefe Memorial Library Fund," named in honor of her dear aunt. Tommy wasn't left out either. Money was set aside for his education, and a computer he wanted.

Shortly before the wedding Alec came over with disturbing news. After Maddy was attacked, he'd made a lot of trips between Nielsen and Omaha concerning the case. After he returned from his last trip he called both Maddy and Aunt Polly to his office.

'Well, we finally figured out who told Fred Simmons about the diary and letters and who hired him to scare you and steal them." Alec's voice was deep and serious, "Leland did overhear us talking and unwittingly told Jack Drake about it."

"Of course, my aunt's attorney, Jack Drake, would have merely had to look in the files. It's the missing piece," Maddy stated, the thread that tied everything together. "The one letter was signed by an attorney named Drake after Al Capone died and left her the bonds. Reginald J. Drake, it was Jack Drake's grandfather."

"No wonder he was so accommodating when he was here. He knew the bonds were still around and worth something. That's a lot of money to lie around in an attic." Aunt Polly said and wiped her glasses.

"He thought he had plenty of time to search, and then I showed up. That must have really shocked him." Maddy leaned forward and shook her head.

"Leland didn't know about Jack Drake's involvement and

innocently told him about the leather case you found in the library, which didn't have anything in it except old receipts."

"What about the body in the truck, this Fred Simmons?" Maddy asked quietly.

"Fred Simmons tried to blackmail Drake for more money."

"How do you know all of this? I mean, are you sure?" Maddy frowned.

"The cowboy's partner, the second guy who stopped you, saw everything. It seems they had a falling out with Jack Drake over money. When they brought him the Al Capone letters and diary it didn't put him any closer to the bonds than before. In fact, it put more heat on than he had expected with the police."

"That's ironic, bad guys blackmailing another bad guy." Maddy said in amazement.

"That's right, and they weren't very good at it. Stealing your aunt's diary and letters was for nothing, too, since the only thing in it was about his father being Al Capone's lawyer."

"You're a good lawman, Alec." Aunt Polly said proudly.

"Thanks Aunt Polly, but it was me and a lot of other law enforcement people working on this case together."

"Did they arrest Jack Drake then?"

"Well, this paper is called a 'death bed' confession." Alec tapped a piece of paper on the palm of his hand and threw it on the desk.

"You're kidding. Jack Drake is dead, too?" Maddy was shocked.

"Died three hours ago. It seems that when he and Simmons argued and wrestled over a gun, it went off killing the guy. Drake had the other one cover it up. Jack Drake had a bad heart and couldn't take the stress after that. They rushed him to the emergency room last night but he didn't make it. He thought it would be a simple case of theft but it turned into murder."

"So it's finally over." Maddy said quietly, a strange feeling of relief coming over her. "I wonder what happened to the letters and the diary."

"Sorry, Maddy, but the second guy said Jack Drake burned them, scared he'd get caught with the evidence. Now you can't prove Al Capone invested the money for your aunt, and I'm sorry about that."

"Oh, that's okay. I have the copies I made for the family history if anyone is interested. The bonds more than make up for that. The library is well on its way to becoming a reality for the town. Tommy is set for life, and the bed and breakfast inn will be open for business right after we get married. I think, considering a gangster started all of this, it's come out pretty good."

"May I make one correction? The inn will start up right after the honeymoon." Alec corrected her.

"Hello? Alec? Oh, Maddy you're all here?" Alec's office door opened a crack and Leland Lancaster peeked in. "I just heard the news about Jack Drake, and I wanted to see if it was true. May I come in?"

"Sure Leland, come in. Yes, it's true if you mean Jack Drake was behind all the trouble for Maddy." Alec leaned back in his chair, arms crossed over his chest.

"I heard Jack's dead." Leland continued. Shock replaced his usual professional demeanor. "I'm so sorry about all the trouble he caused you, you could have been killed. I didn't know he was doing that, I swear."

"We know that, Leland. Please, don't worry about it." Maddy was sorry to see him so upset.

"I introduced him to your aunt, Miss Morris and he was my attorney too, the best in the state, I thought. It looks like he embezzled from a lot of his clients. How wrong can a guy get?"

"Leland, he fooled a lot of people. No one's blaming you." Maddy said softly.

"I suppose. Thanks for saying that. It's turned out okay though. I hear Miss Madeline's money is going to start a new library?"

"Well, yes, it did turn out okay. And it brought Alec and me together, too." Maddy slipped her arm around Alec's waist, smiling broadly as she flashed her engagement ring proudly.

"That wasn't hard to see, I knew it right off. I hope I'm invited to the wedding?" Leland asked coyly.

"You're first on the list, Leland, after Aunt Polly, of course." Maddy patted his arm.

"I knew it all along. I'd be honored to attend. We'll be seeing you at the church, then. Good by Aunt Polly." He winked as he slipped out the door.

"He never had a clue about the two of you," Aunt Polly snorted and then laughed. "Oh, well, like he said, it's a small town and word gets around."

The wedding went beautifully. All present agreed that the ceremony was exceptionally nice. Along with all the traditionally wrapped presents, one in particular Maddy steered Alec to open.

Highly suspicious, Alec carefully looked at the big, blue bow around a sturdy box.

"It won't explode, will it? I think we've had enough mystery for a while." He teased.

Maddy urged him on and Alec tore back the lid and found a rollicking, gangly puppy inside. With joy on his face, he happily pointed a finger at his new wife.

"Hey, you remembered, and she's a hunting dog."

"He. It's a he, and he's a purebred. German Shorthaired Pointer, Bubba said you always liked them."

"What a great gift. Just what I wanted. Thank you. How you doing there, Buddy? Gee, guess he needs a name. What shall we call him, Maddy?"

"That's easy." Maddy smiled coyly and pulled a dog food bowl from behind her. The big, red letters on the bowl read simply, *AL.*

~End~

About the Author

Author Kathleen Pieper was born and raised in Nebraska. At the age of 8 she wrote her first book and from then on it [life] was all about the written word. She still shows this book when she give talks to school kids. From little Golden Books, Nancy Drew series and early romance novels, she was hooked on reading and writing.

A native Nebraskan, she retired with her husband to their hometown of Grand Island where they now live with two hunting dogs, surrounded by family and old friends. She was a stay-at-home mom before it was popular and it worked out well giving her time to write four novels published by Avalon Publishers.

Her fifth book, *"Letters From Al"* is inspired by an old photograph the author was drawn to as a child at her grandmother's house. It was of her great aunt Sophia, and the image drifted in and out of her life until her aging grandmother gave her the photo. Visions and ideas sprang to life in the story of an unknown flapper and Al Capone, the gangster. That's how *Letters from Al,* a romantic mystery, was born.

In 2010 she placed second in the NE State Mother's Assn. short story contest, and first in the National Mother's of America contest. She is a member of the Nebraska Writer's Guild, Romance Writer's of America, Prairieland Romance Writer's group and The Grand Island Critiquers. Her hobbies include reading, crafting and enjoying her family which has grown to include grandchildren.